DOUBLE EXPOSURE

A F/NBI ENEMIES-TO-LOVERS
ROMANTIC SUSPENSE

RIEN GRAY

DOUBLE EXPOSURE

RIEN GRAY

CONTENT NOTES

This book contains explicit sexual content and is intended for readers over 18 years of age. All characters portrayed in these acts are consenting adults. There are brief references to societal transphobia, historical anti-Black racism in Chicago, class discrimination, and exploitation of the opioid epidemic, as well as one incident of gun violence.

CHAPTER I
JILLIAN

S tealing is like falling in love.
Whether the desire sparks at first sight or burns
down slow, chasing after who and what you want is
second nature. Chemistry and opportunity isn't always
enough; you have to make an impact—and ensure whoever
finds out about the theft gets so jealous they can't see
straight. By risking everything and succeeding, you become
the type of person they write songs and screenplays about, a
paragon of the perfect catch.

I'm not sure if Russell Key Jr. is my type yet. In a physical
sense, I would pass: his five-o'clock shadow holds more
desperation than charisma, and a sheaf of blonde hair has
survived a few uneven cuts, taking on an oily sheen each
time he brushes thin bangs back behind square black glasses.

His background is equally unimpressive. The sons of
celebrities rarely outshine their parents, and Russell is no
exception. Thirty years of life has resulted in a half-finished
art degree, the barebones brownstone in which I'm presently

sitting, and a host of appearances in low-budget documentaries and reality shows.

Everything he's said since I walked in the door, though? My interest is piqued.

"I want my father's photos back," Russell mutters, smudging a new fingerprint onto his lenses. "No matter what it takes."

"Why these pictures in particular?" I gesture to the framed magazine covers next to us: *Rolling Stone, GQ, TIME.* "Your father took thousands of photographs and sold most of them. That money went right to you when he died."

Irritation wrinkles Russell's brow. "He didn't *sell* these. They were discovered right after Dad died. Someone dug them up in an apartment he owned."

Ah, that rings a bell. "His little hideaway in Brazil, right? If I recall correctly, everything your father printed in that era was... salacious."

Russell winces. "Yeah. He was having an affair."

Not just any affair. Adriana Azevedo was Miss Rio de Janeiro in 1990, and slated for Miss Brasil the same year until her mysterious disappearance. Mr. Key ended up arrested on suspicion for her murder before he quietly ducked out of the country. Authorities let the case drop, but Adriana never resurfaced.

It's the sort of scandal that earned months of press back in the day but barely registers now. If not for the fact Key made his name photographing some of the most controversial figures of the era, this story would be decades-old tabloid grist.

"And you want me to *recover*—" I use careful verbiage with clients, because you never know when guilt will get the better of them. "—an entire collection of images where your father is clearly having sex with a woman who isn't your mother."

Russell slumps forward, shoulders bearing in. "I know my dad was a screwed-up guy. The Hunter S. Thompson of photography or whatever."

Quite the reach, considering Thompson took plenty of pictures himself. "I'm not judging, Russell. But if I were you, I'd never want to see those photos again."

"I don't have a choice." Blue eyes flash with anger. "The Art Institute of Chicago is about to show the collection off to the whole world and sell tickets. They stole those photos from my mother."

Another point in his favor—I love one-upping other thieves. "Stole how?"

He sags back into his chair, an old leather beast leaning far more to his father's aesthetic than his own. "Dad died, right? Mom was grieving, and then his old landlord in Brazil found that box of photos in some weird hidden drawer under the bed and sent them to her. Instantly, we have press banging down our door. Fans begging to buy the pictures. We hadn't even buried him yet. The day we do, some museum administrator shows up at the funeral and talks her into giving up the pictures. Saying he'd 'honor my father's legacy' *and* her privacy. Guess that didn't take."

I'm a loner, but I do my best not to be tactless. Still, it's worth mentioning the obvious. "Your mother passed last year, Russell."

"Yeah." His shoulders tighten, curling in like a beetle. "So now she can't have second thoughts about the Institute putting up everything on display. They didn't pay my mother a single red cent. She never wanted those pictures shown to the public, but the thought of destroying art Dad made..."

Russell shakes his head. "Point is, the museum won't give

9

them up. I've offered everything I have. Last time I called, they threatened to get a restraining order."

Which means Key's reputation is about to get a very explicit revival. Anyone holding onto his work in private collections will get a boost too, opening up the floor for auctions in the millions. Most major museums have their hands in both sectors—legally or otherwise—and are bound to benefit from the attention, taking a cut from whatever sales exchange hands. By cold capitalist logic, I'm not surprised they turned Russell down. The leftover royalties from his inheritance are pennies in comparison.

But I work on commission, and if the piece sounds like a fun steal, I'm open to sliding scale. Lucky for the sad man sitting in front of me, the Institute recently purchased a top-of-the-line security system that apparently no one has been able to bypass. Walking off with anything inside their walls would be worth bragging about—taking Key's most infamous but never-before-seen photos before they can be displayed to the public would turn whoever stole them into a legend.

The only thing I enjoy more than a good payday is proving I'm the best in the business.

"You understand that you'll be their first suspect when the pictures go missing," I say.

"Jillian." Russell smiles; unfortunately, it's as charming as roadkill in the rain. "Or Jill, if you prefer—"

"Jillian. Nothing else." The denial comes out harsher than I intend. Nicknames piss me off. "But you were saying?"

"I know I'll be a suspect." He shrugs. "But the second you hand them over, I'm going to burn everything. They can arrest me, but they can't undo that."

Huh. Russell has more steel in his spine than I gave him credit for. Setting art ablaze puts a reflexive knot of disgust deep in my gut, but if someone was about to show off photos of my loved one fucking to a legion of tourists, I'd break out the lighter too.

"Fair enough, but you're not the only one at risk." Theft of a major artwork—either a century old or worth more than a hundred grand—carries a ten year prison sentence, not counting whatever breaking and entering charges get tacked on in the mix. Add a dose of conspiracy, and the recipe is life behind bars. "Why should I trust you, Russell? What stops you from turning me in to get a better deal?"

One watery eye twitches, instantly nervous. He looks down at his hands as if it will hide the reflex, but fear leaves him sallow with sweat. "I... hell, I don't know. I can promise that I won't, or give you half the cash upfront—"

"How much cash?" I interrupt.

Russell straightens up. "Five hundred grand. I have it right... uh."

He hesitates, clearly realizing he was about to advertise where half a million dollars is hiding to a near stranger, but enough zeroes are on the table that I don't mind. The pictures would sell for ten times more if a buyer could be found, but trafficking a collection that hot takes so many years and third parties it isn't worth the trouble. Every new link in the chain is a chance to get caught; one of many reasons I'm a solo operator, even if that means having to meet with clients myself.

"If the money is close, you can get it to the drop point I specify within twelve hours. If I receive the cash in time, and I'm given no reason to distrust you, then I'll accept the job. Extraction should be in under two weeks."

Excitement gets the better of him, putting a slick shine on blue eyes, but Russell tries to rein it back in with a frown. "What's stopping you from robbing me of half a mill?"

I smile. My personal safe has more money in it than someone like him has ever seen, but bragging is a loser's game. Keeping an edge in negotiations is always worth more than pride. If Russell is going to back out, this is the moment.

"Nothing," I say. "Trust goes both ways."

"Shit." He flinches, running a hand back through his hair again. "You're sure you can do it? Steal the photos out from under the Institute's nose?"

"Who said anything about stealing?" Entrapment is hard to prove, but I still prefer not to advertise so openly. "Those pictures belong to your family. I just want to see everything returned to its rightful place. After that, it's not my business what happens."

Russell is silent for a stretch of heartbeats. He's terrified, but that's fine by me; people who are absolutely sure they can get away with a crime are always the ones who break the second something goes wrong. Fear breeds caution, and I'm good at keeping a leash on both. Get a client invested, and they'll believe you're the only thing that can keep them safe —or a ghost who can walk off with everything they've ever loved. Betrayal is out of the question.

So I wait, matching his silence with my own, until Russell lets out a deep breath and nods. "Okay. Yeah, let's do it."

I reach into my purse and pull out a flat black notebook along with my favorite pen: a custom Montblanc with a grip made of unfinished blackwood. The inkwell takes an age to run dry, and good luck getting fingerprints off such a rough surface.

"Write down everything in here that you know about the photos, your father, the museum. Even your mother. However small or insignificant the detail, I want to know."

Russell takes the notebook but gives me a curious look. "I'll wait. If it takes days, so be it."

"Why?" he asks. "Can't I call or—"

"No. After today, you won't ever contact me again. That number is already disconnected. I'll take the cash with a dead drop, and the photos will be delivered to you just the same." I lean forward, ensuring Russell can see my eyes over my sunglasses, dead serious. "Don't even think my name. I don't exist, and we've never met. Is that clear?"

His Adam's apple bobs. "Crystal."

Russell whips open the cover of the notebook and starts writing in a quick, left-handed scrawl, but after about five minutes of peace, he cocks his head and frowns.

"Do you hear that?" he asks. "Like a super low buzzing sound."

"No," I lie.

The white noise app running on my phone is buried deep in my purse, whispering interference into the air. Too many good thieves have been undone by a cell phone or recording device hidden just out of reach. I refuse to take the risk.

He shrugs off his own concern and starts writing again. It takes the better part of an hour—during which Russell awkwardly offers me a beer, then wine, both of which I refuse—and almost a dozen double-sided pages before he hands the pen and notebook back.

I scan for anything out of the ordinary. Plenty of useful personal information jumps out, more than enough for me to copy Russell's identity on the fly, but emptying out someone's bank account is nowhere near as satisfying as stealing art. Over the years, I've tried almost every con and trick, and little compares to having a thousand year old statue taking up a body's worth of space in a hotel room, or walking off with a ten million dollar painting like it's a stick of gum from the corner store.

Getting paid to do the deed is therapeutic, really.

"Everything seems to be in order." I return the pen to my purse and snap the notebook shut. "Goodbye, Russell. It's been a pleasure doing business. You'll receive the coordinates for the payment after I'm gone."

He flashes a weak smile; it doesn't meet his eyes. "Nice to meet you too."

Definitely not my type. Confidence is social lubricant in more ways than one.

Russell blurts out a "thanks!" as I leave the brownstone, but I don't bother to reply. Step one is reconnaissance, and I'd like to have the ball rolling before the cash is even in hand. Call it professional pride.

Which means I have a date with a pretty museum in Chicago, and she'll be waiting for me to discover all of her dirty little secrets.

CHAPTER 2
SLOANE

S tealing is like sex.

The adrenaline, the anticipation, countless moves chasing pleasure until getting what you really want. Whether it's a one-night stand or a regular hookup, the taking alone isn't what satisfies. Feeling out boundaries until the balance of power shifts, and for a few perfect seconds, you're vulnerable—or you're a god. If luck holds, the feeling lasts longer, but either way, you'll be back for another taste soon enough.

And everyone panics if you do it in public.

Thomas Zouch is a triple-digit millionaire, but even a bathtub full of diamonds couldn't talk me into bed with him. Thankfully, our relationship is strictly platonic: he calls me, I fly across the ocean to England, and we discuss what he wants me to steal and how much he's going to give me for it.

The ten-hour flight might look like a power play, but when the ticket is on Thomas' dime, I don't mind. Meeting in person means reading his body language without the details getting lost in translation, and every time I visit, I map out another room of Thomas' self-styled manor. He bought his peerage from the British government in the early nineties and spent the last thirty years bribing officials to convince the public his title was gifted out of bloodline legitimacy.

I couldn't possibly care less, but I am looking forward to robbing him of every last penny one day. Maybe it's my American upbringing or whatever Irish lineage lingers in my veins, but the very concept of a noble class fills me with the kind of rage that imprints the recipe for firebombs into ancestral memory.

Oh, well. His time will come.

"Sloane!" A pale, wrinkled hand pats my shoulder as Thomas guides me to a chair, carved and set one inch shorter than his own. Money can't fix insecurity. "How was the jump across the pond?"

First class. "I slept. It's the only way to beat jet lag."

He settles into his own seat, gripping the overstuffed burgundy arms like a king holding court. "I miss traveling. So much business here at home, you know."

What I know is Thomas doesn't pay me enough for small talk. "What are you after this time? Need another painting for the fireplace?"

"For such a good thief, you're dreadfully impatient." His graying brow crinkles. "No updates about your life? New house? New woman? Or women, plural, I suppose. I don't judge."

Not to my face, anyway. Thomas has always struck me as the type to say "queer" like it burned his tongue. "None of the above. Business is great, but I can't keep my reputation if I get distracted."

He accepts the subtle barb with a sigh, then reaches over to his side table to grab a heavy book. One of those talking pieces in a wraparound cover, showing a grizzled but smiling man staring at a bloodied, haunted doppelgänger. *Kill Your Idols: The Thousand Faces of Russell Key* is emblazoned across the front in white block print.

Thomas holds up the book. "Do you know his work?"

Only because Key's cock and his camera intersected more often than not. "Sure. Russell put a mirror in front of a lot of famous people, and they liked him. He thought he was a rock star, and went out like one—sex, drugs, getting away with murder."

He clears his throat. "Well, Key was never convicted. And his multiple exposure techniques were quite revolutionary for the era. The problem is, he liked to burn his negatives after finishing a piece and bartered his pictures for everything from cars to cocaine."

"Which makes his remaining work valuable." By a certain standard, anyway. "But I've seen Key's photos go up for auction before, Thomas. They sell well, but you usually ask me to go after bigger fish."

The baron prefers classic art, painted or sculpted by people who have been dead for a hundred years or more. Age keeps the value high, and pop culture can't reclaim what's never allowed to fall in its hands in the first place. Thomas has a vault hermetically sealed away from the world that would make any historian break down in tears. I've talked my way into collections on five continents on his behalf and carried out enough priceless artifacts to fill my own museum, but most of my targets have no clue what they've lost. Making fakes is easy when provenance goes unchecked for years on end. Why let an expert put their hands all over your gallery when you're already sure everything inside is real?

"The photos I want aren't for sale, and they're *much* bigger fish." Thomas sets the book aside, then folds both hands in his lap. "The Art Institute of Chicago is about to exhibit a hidden collection of Key's. They acquired six unique pictures quite some time ago, only to put them into storage immediately. Some business about not wanting to upset his wife."

That rings a bell. "Didn't she die a while back?"

"Apparently, a year is the polite amount of time to wait after a woman's death before publishing proof of her husband's most infamous affair." A dry chuckle leaves Thomas' throat. Idly, I wish he would choke. "Only a few people in the entire world have seen these photographs, Sloane. And I would like to keep it that way."

"By transferring these photos from the Institute's collection to yours?" I ask.

Satisfaction hoods gray eyes, leaving him looking a bit like a toad who hasn't realized the water around it is about to hit a boil. "Yes. I know I don't usually give you a time limit, but this is a rather special case."

I wouldn't work with Thomas if I didn't enjoy a challenge. "When does the collection go up for public consumption?"

"A week from now." When I frown, he holds up a hand to stall. "A tight deadline, I know. But the Institute administration has kept this very hush-hush. They're hoping a surprise release will stimulate ticket sales."

Not to mention a sudden boost in reputation. Everyone wants to go viral these days; tourists and influencers will be breaking down the museum's doors to get a taste of fame by proxy. Add in the fact that most of Key's pictures border on the pornographic, and the controversy is designed to sell itself into an ouroboros of attention.

But the thief who steals the photos and gets away with

it? They would be the best in the world, and I have a vested interest in keeping that title.

Details first, though. "Doesn't Russell Key have a son? What does he think about Daddy Dearest's business getting flashed around?"

Thomas brushes off the question with an imperious huff. "Nothing relevant. He's been riding his father's coattails a very long time, but he has no claim to the photographs."

"Really?" Most valuable pieces are leased to various institutions in return for getting to plaster one's name across the exhibit. "How did that happen?"

"Marisa Key surrendered the full property rights when she was alive. She didn't want anything to do with those images." He smiles, teeth too clean. "I appreciate the value of a good scandal, but it's funny to make such a big deal about a naked photographer and his girlfriend when the old Greco-Roman statues have been tits out for decades."

The quirk his accent puts on 'tits out' earns a real laugh out of me. "I won't argue that. But I am careful about provenance, Thomas. You know that."

"Yes, you want art in the *proper* hands." A touch of disdain laces his words, although Thomas tries to keep his smile intact. "But Key Jr. isn't an exploited tribe or vulnerable nation plundered for its riches. He's just a boy living in his father's shadow."

Fair game then, I suppose. About half of my work is pro bono, returning works stolen during world wars and the sort of colonial conquest everyone pretends doesn't happen anymore. I was raised by people like Thomas, leeches who see the sick and starving as little more than an easy meal, no matter how many lives are lost or destroyed by their gluttony. To say money isn't why I do this isn't quite true: I just want wealth in the hands of those who need it most, which sometimes requires hands-on redistribution.

After a certain point, being rich eats away empathy, one cruel bite at a time. So I take enough for my expenses and pass on the rest. Squeezing every last cent out of my paying clients is its own pleasure, though. They're welcome to exploit each other as much as they like.

"And my fee?"

Thomas' mouth tightens into a thin line. He finds it uncouth that I talk about money in direct terms, rather than playing a game of gratitude. I don't need him, but he needs me, and I'll never let him forget it.

"Two million," he suggests after a moment of silence.

Wow. Getting more than six digits out of Thomas usually takes two blackmail threats, a promise to walk out the door, and a cup of awful British tea while he fusses over the numbers. He *really* wants these pictures. "Half up front."

"A quarter up front," Thomas counters. There's the tight-fisted bastard I know. "You usually break into private vaults or closed collections. I don't want to throw away a million dollars and end up embarrassed."

"You don't trust my expertise?" When he opens his mouth to protest, I interrupt. "Because I imagine you're not the only bidder interested in Key's work. It would be just as easy for me to take the pictures and put up my own little auction."

His mouth crumples into a frown. "Pettiness doesn't suit you, Sloane."

Well, that's ridiculous. I started my entire career by being petty. "Forty percent. In cash. And it's in my hands before I fly home."

"Deal." Thomas holds up a finger in warning. "But the rest is only if you get every single photograph in that collection before the public sees them and deliver the collection personally."

I've always done dead drops; even with established clients like Thomas, best practices are force of habit. A cop or customs official getting suspicious at just the wrong moment is how most thieves get caught, lost in the haze of business as usual.

"You don't care about the pictures at all, do you?" I ask. "They could show a dog pissing itself and you'd pay the same amount of money to make sure they were off limits to the cheap seats."

My crude metaphor earns a grimace, but Thomas' answer proves the point at hand. "What value is there in owning what everyone else has?"

Nothing, to a man like him. "I should get going if I'm going to make your timeline, then. Any other pressing factors?"

Thomas reaches for the photobook again. The pages whisper against one another before he pulls out a piece of paper hidden between them and hands it to me. "The name of the Institute's administrator. He also has a daughter in her twenties, if you would prefer to gain access that way."

Depends on which side of her twenties she's on. I don't rob the cradle, job or not. A shining public reputation is one of the most useful tools in my arsenal; appearing pleasant, timely, and wealthy is better than any lockpick or hacksaw. Some thieves break through doors—I make sure they're opened for me.

I take Thomas' note. *Clayton Woodward* is flanked by a phone number, with *Ella Woodward* scribbled underneath. "Great doing business, Thomas. I'll see you in a week."

He smiles and rises from his chair. "Let me escort you to the door."

Thomas has paid help for such trifles, but even our longstanding business relationship can't repel the unease of having a known thief wandering around the house unattended. He knows I can talk anyone into almost anything. The amusing part is his surety in being immune.

Brisk London air welcomes me as the manor door clicks shut with the weight of Scots pine and brass. A quick check on my phone offers up the next flight to Chicago three hours from now, so I book a ticket and flag down a taxi to take me to the airport. With international boarding times, I'll be cutting it close.

Once I'm back on my side of the map, the first order of business is a little recon.

CHAPTER 3
JILLIAN

General admission to the Art Institute of Chicago costs twenty-five dollars a ticket. I buy a multi-day fastpass for a hundred because the package comes with free storage for my purse, including the live recording device inside. Its technology is remarkably sensitive, sure to pick up chatter from the security booth nearby and the museum radio positioned right behind the counter. Two hours should cover the average guard rotation, so I can review the audio file later and confirm whatever codes they use with one another.

Visitors have three entrances to choose from, but their construction is similar: glass doors glazed to resist the cruel spectrum of Illinois weather, surrounded by clear double-paned frames protecting against the same. The main thoroughfare—angled against the gift shop—is flanked by a pair of massive bronze lions, hides gone green after decades of exposure to sun and rain. Whenever one of the local sports teams wins a championship, they put the beasts in matching jerseys and helmets.

Admittedly, it's kind of cute.

My fastpass is accepted with a scan and a glance by a guard in her twenties, brunette and a touch too narrow for her uniform, which billows around her shoulders and ribs. She straightens up when our eyes meet, confirming my disguise is in full effect.

A wide-brimmed hat, impenetrable black sunglasses, and nude Serge Lutens lipstick to imply taste without an eye-catching color. The dress I'm wearing is a sheath of cool blue linen, perfect for the two weeks a year when Chicago doesn't freeze or burn. It even has pockets. Well-off but anonymous is the intention, someone who views a museum as a shopping list rather than a day's entertainment.

I break from the entryway crowd and step into a massive Barbara Kreuger exhibit. The billboard outside boasted her mixed-medium pieces sprawl over eighteen thousand square feet, designed with assistance from the artist. Massive green Xs cover the floor, blotting out Kreuger's own words imprinted on the tile and leading to hallways of her vinyls and videos, punctuated with pieces filling the entire museum with letters bigger than my torso.

Camera coverage is minimal once I'm past the first stretch of exhibits. The reason besuited escorts stand at the entryway of every wing and auditorium is because CCTV is an expensive enterprise, with batteries and wires offering an ever-present threat to anything displayed underneath them. Even the most famous museums rarely retain the budget for twenty-four hour scrutiny, which is why I'm curious what new toy the Institute purchased to protect Key's photos.

With several floors and endless hallways, it takes a few rounds before I find the blank white walls signaling an exhibit in progress. The gap is in their Contemporary Art section, which fits, and several temporary frames—I count six—have been outlined with blue painter's tape on the walls above a smooth concrete floor. I spy one camera, but it's pointing toward the elevator, and while the glass doors to this room are presently shut, it would be impossible to see inside while standing at either the front or back of the hallway.

Two motion detectors hide in the far corners of the exhibit, but their lights are off, presumably not to disturb cleaners or the construction crew. Key's photos must be in the Institute's vault at the moment, sealed behind half a dozen keycard-seeking locks and granite walls meant to impede drills and earthquakes alike. Standard procedure says the museum will bring them up a few days in advance, allowing for seventy-two hours of arguments about what should be positioned where.

I could crack the vault, but it's a far busier space where more extreme security measures take hold. The average museum only shows off five percent of their collection at once, and their budget is better spent protecting the majority. Stealing underground is a risky endeavor anyway; if I can't always see an exit into open air, I can't guarantee my escape.

So this room is my new territory. Today is about getting the lay of the land, measurements included.

Certain thieves talk their way into a space, socially engineering an opportunity to be alone with their intended target before sneaking their prize out. "Soft" skills, as it were. I can con with the top brass, but in my opinion, stealing something is much easier when the fewest possible number of people are involved. Why say a word to security when I can slip inside unnoticed, take what's mine, and leave without a single alarm being tripped?

The notebook I keep tucked away is half the size of my

palm and bound to its own little pencil. My private shorthand doesn't need much space, and the entire set is small enough to burn with fifteen seconds and a sixty-cent lighter. I take down details on relevant features: physical dimensions, visible construction materials, and the buttons inside the elevator.

One of them is unlabeled, black, and requires a key before it can even be pressed. I can only assume it provides access to the vault; they wouldn't be caught hauling priceless works of art up and down the stairs. This particular car is weighted for up to eight thousand pounds, another subtle confirmation.

I reach into my pocket and remove a slender chunk of molding plaster, rolled out to the size of a cigarette. Once the plastic is stripped off, it's easy to work the soft putty into the lock. It dries hard in seconds, allowing me to pull out a raw copy of the key. This little clone would break if I tried to turn it, but the outline is more than enough to make a functional duplicate back at my hotel room.

Before leaving, I triple-check the expiration date on the maintenance certificate inside the elevator. Get stuck in a steel box once during a heist and it stays with you forever. I learned how to climb up and down industrial shafts after that.

"Ma'am?" A voice comes from my left as I step back into the gallery; I affix a polite smile to my face. "Are you lost?"

The culprit is a pasty man with graying hair and a remarkably flat face, like someone let a clay figurehead hit the floor before throwing it in the kiln. His short burgundy jacket, unbuttoned to let the barrel of his belly breathe, marks him as a docent. Which means no gun like the rent-a-cops keeping watch in the vault below, but a coin toss as to whether or not he'll have the same overblown sense of authority.

Better to look vulnerable either way. "Yes, actually. I was looking for the stairs to the Greco-Roman section, but I can't seem to find them."

He smiles and gestures behind me. "That elevator will take you right up there. Just go up one floor."

"It has to be stairs." I let my smile fall, adding a beleaguered sigh. "My doctor told me to get as much cardio as possible. Terrible heart problems run in the family."

Hazel eyes round in sympathy; chances are I was right about the subtle bump in his shirt being a pacemaker. "I'm afraid the only stairs around here are for emergencies or employees only, but I can point you in the right direction."

Good to know there's another way out. "Please. I'd really appreciate it."

After following him out of the empty hall, I mark the little green emergency exit sign, legally required despite the nearly invisible door it's attached to. A hint of dust around the base implies the thoroughfare isn't well-used, but without being able to see through to the other side, confirming exactly which floors this stairwell connects to is impossible. Which is fine—I'll find out for myself after losing my escort and circling back around.

The crossroads between exhibits is packed now, thanks to two different high school field trips colliding with patrons from the Institute's café. For a second, all I can smell is coffee and sweat; a fine combination when you wake up in bed with someone the morning after exhausting each other with pleasure, brutal when spilling out of a mass of bodies.

I can't wait to have this entire building to myself. The only light will be the moon through glass and regulated constellations of green dots, marking alarms, keypads, and temperature control. I know how to walk on tile without making a sound, so nothing will tear the cloak of perfect silence pulled over long wings of artwork, showcasing centuries of beauty, politics, culture, and skill. Millions of dollars sitting in plain view, arranged to draw the eye—and the hand. Who among us hasn't wanted to touch something so valuable, so precious, so rare?

"Take this flight up and you'll find everything you're looking for," the docent says.

He honestly seems happy to be of service, so I smile again. Standing watch in the same ten doorways ensuring handsy teenagers don't accidentally elbow the original *American Gothic* can only inspire Sisyphean levels of boredom. "Thank you very much, sir."

The 'sir' catches him off-guard. He straightens and bows his head with a solemnity I usually only see in the South—a formative upbringing that never quite let go. In that sense, I can relate, although I'd rather die than go back to the stark red deserts of Arizona, too poor for air conditioning and starved for opportunity. "My pleasure, ma'am."

Once he's gone, I count the windows in the skylight above me and add that number to the notebook. Ground-level entry is my preference, but sometimes dropping down in one fell swoop to the bottom of a building is easier rather than bypassing several sets of doors. An antenna sits at the very top that I can't get a read on, but the highest point looks clear of cameras, which puts several points in that plan's favor.

Maybe the Institute doesn't have the money for constant surveillance, but I do. First thing tomorrow, I'll come back and plant a quiet little bug in the corner of the Contemporary Art section, then watch the feed from my hotel room until the photos are taken out of storage.

Between that footage and whatever gossip I'm about to collect from the cocked ear in my purse, every secret behind their supposedly invulnerable security will be mine.

I turn back toward the Contemporary wing and bump against someone. Recognition splits the details into snapshots: a bespoke Zegna suit, slate gray, no tie; a perfect V of skin from collarbone to throat flanked by open pearl buttons; a full, imperious mouth and the fine bridge of a nose once broken but set perfectly; tennis court green eyes and a crown of long, lustrous red hair thick enough to sink a fist into.

The bastard who broke my heart is standing right in front of me.

They crack a smile. "Long time no see, jewel."

CHAPTER 4

SLOANE

Have you ever had a woman try to drive you personally, deliberately insane?

Jillian Rhodes could do anything with her prodigious intelligence and expertise: run for political office, become a CIA agent, blackmail a king into giving her an island. What she *has* done is steal approximately a hundred million dollars in art all on her lonesome, and yet somehow finds time in that remarkably busy schedule to fuck me over at every conceivable opportunity. After three consecutive years of screwing, I've gotten pretty good at revenge, but she is the last person I want to see while planning a heist like this.

"It's Jillian." The cold snap in her voice puts the Arctic shelf to shame. "Not 'jewel', not 'Jill'. Jillian. Use my name properly or keep it out of your mouth."

None of my best answers to that should be heard by the pair of teenagers sharing a soda next to us, so I settle for, "It used to be your favorite."

I wish she was less beautiful. There should be some sign

the last three years have done even a fraction of as much damage to her as they did to me, but she stands untouched by time. Jillian has to look up to meet my eyes, and past the dark shield of on-brand sunglasses, hers are a piercing hazel, like golden flecks on agarwood. Her hair is pulled back tight under a derby hat, hiding the color from any cameras above, but I can see the burnished gold hasn't changed a bit—no strands of gray, no loss of sheen. A face full of understated makeup means nothing distracts from her sinuous mouth, smooth skin, or a porcelain jaw that could have been sculpted by one of the Old Masters.

"Now that's old news, isn't it?" Loathing turns Jillian's gaze wolfish. "How was Milan?"

Last month, Milan was where a broker for the local Stidda crime family inadvertently revealed one of Tiziano Vecelli's—Titian, for the English—masterpieces had ended up in his custody. The Venice museum that owned the painting went hunting for it, but legal options are limited whenever the Mafia gets involved.

I took a commission fee for the painting's recovery under an alias, but my exit plan was interrupted by a bellboy at the hotel using my real name when he came to pick up the luggage where I'd stashed the Titian. The broker was a single phone call from siccing his made men on me before I secured another escape route. Only one person knows which hotels I frequent in Italy—and would drop a helpful tip to the concierge at just the wrong moment.

"Profitable," I say, eyes narrowing. "Did you enjoy Hong Kong?"

Irritation flutters across her brow. "I'll have my visa back soon enough."

Good luck. I informed the local embassy she was there under false pretenses, and they don't take kindly to lying

Americans. New gray and black markets pop up in Asia every day, spearheaded by exploitative expats who know rich investors back West will pay top dollar to avoid both government scrutiny and customs fees. Cutting off Jillian from any of those avenues is a direct blow to her career in both the short and long term.

Before Hong Kong, our battleground was sculptures in Dublin. Before Dublin, we sparred over a piece of Greek black figure pottery with three separate claims of provenance. After she got me arrested in Barcelona, all bets were off. I struck back in Manila, Tokyo, and the Maldives. To the average Interpol officer, Jillian's complete lie of a cover story is worth little scrutiny—too many actual American heiresses coast along on money from industries built back in World War II—but I've memorized her quirks and tells. When she's about to steal something, it echoes in my bones.

"What brings you to Chicago?" I ask.

I don't expect a real answer, but it's impossible not to wonder. After three years of trading blows from a distance, seeing Jillian in person again is like taking a cattle prod to the spine. While I enjoy games of power, pain has never been to my taste.

"As if I'd tell you." Jillian's lips quirk, breaking the perfect symmetry of her face. "Or maybe I should. Would you take me at my word?"

Once upon a time? Always. We promised to be honest with each other, regardless of the cost. "I'm just curious what made you decide to start doing your dirty work face-to-face again. Did you finally get lonely, Jill?"

One of Jillian's hands clenches into a fist at her side, the threat barely restrained. She's remarkably strong for her size; a decade of scaling buildings and slipping through vents has that effect on a woman.

Which is why her being here doesn't make any sense. Jillian is a thief of the classic break-and-enter methodology, sabotaging security systems and reputedly impassable vaults. The Institute has its own labyrinth down below full of art in storage, but that's always been true. What could have changed to attract the attention of someone like her, hungry to challenge herself against the most difficult locks and alarms?

Whatever it is, the piece must be valuable. Jillian doesn't get out of bed for anything less than six figures.

"No matter what you've deluded yourself into believing, my life does not revolve around you, Caffrey." She whispers, but the quiet is somehow twice as hostile, a knife stabbing out of the dark. "I'm sure you're here to play an idiot with more wealth than sense and simper until someone falls for the most embarrassing con in existence, but I don't care. Just stay out of my way."

"Out of *your* way?" How fucking rich. "Unless this is your idea of a vacation, go back to your little spy nest and eavesdrop on people with actual lives. Maybe if you do it long enough, that rusty piece of scrap you call a heart will find some empathy. You might even turn into a real girl, if you're lucky."

Her head snaps down, and between the hat and sunglasses, Jillian's expression is beyond my reach. "Even if I did, you wouldn't be worth a single minute of my time."

Bold words for someone who gives me more of her time than anyone else. "I'm heartbroken. Truly. But if I'm staying out of your way, you're staying out of mine. Start playing games and I'll bury you."

"If you'd ever held a shovel in your life, that would be terrifying." She steps past me, close enough to touch but holding the distance. "Let's never do this again, shall we? Goodbye."

Jillian dives into the crowd with an Olympian's silent grace, but I watch until she falls out of sight completely. Back toward the Contemporary Art wing, which is notable; she's not a creator or a collector, even on the side. Jillian doesn't just steal because the trade is what she's best at, but because it gives her access to independence nothing else can promise. When you're as good as she is, the risk is almost completely sublimated by reward.

I used to find that confidence attractive, but the other side of the mirror is arrogance, the belief that she has the right to alter the world around her on a whim, regardless of who it hurts. What Jillian declares to be cold but sensible logic is a mask for a selfish, egotistical id that she spoils rotten. I know her background, but that's no excuse; at thirty-three years old, everyone is accountable for their actions.

Whatever. I have work to do, and I won't let Jillian's overblown grudge become a distraction.

My first stop is the information booth, positioned like a panopticon near Barbara Kruger's *I love myself and you hate me for it*. The words tower in deep monochrome cuts over a blonde guard, LOVE punctuated by the green of a brand-new traffic light. She doesn't seem to mind the decoration, eyes flickering over the passing crowd, lingering on long coats and high schoolers moving in packs: the usual suspects. They're easy trouble, more prone to vandalism than theft, although the ambitious can escalate quickly.

I would know—I set a billion dollars ablaze on my eighteenth birthday.

"Miss?" Two steps forward break the guard's line of sight; I summon an apologetic smile before her attention snaps to my face. The black plastic tab of her name tag reads *Olivia*. "Could I ask for some directions? I've gotten completely turned around."

Gray eyes sweep me again, appreciative, teeth edging against her lip before she clears her throat. "Ahem. Of course. Where are you trying to go?"

"I have a meeting with Director Woodward." I lean in, voice soft and conspiratorial. "He told me his office was near the Kruger exhibit, but..."

"She's decorating the entire museum." Olivia laughs. "Woodward is on the third floor, next to the sculpture terrace. King of the castle, you can't miss him."

The key to getting information out of people is starting with simple questions, ones they answer by reflex. Telling a stranger the obvious feels harmless, but when we're primed to be helpful, secrets start to slip out with ease. One thread feeds into another, and as soon as I have enough of them wrapped around my fingers, unraveling someone takes a single, calculated tug.

"Thanks." She leans into my gratitude without thinking, a sunflower following the light. "You wouldn't happen to know what he's exhibiting on Friday, would you? Clayton's been teasing me about it for a month."

Olivia's jaw tightens, a flicker of caution. "You're not a journalist, are you?"

I glance down, drawing the angle of her attention to my suit. "People usually write articles about me, not the other way around."

"Oh, I didn't—" She searches my face, hungry for recognition and finding nothing, as intended. I keep a wide berth from real reporters, although a few of my thefts have splashed onto the front page of various newspapers. "I'm so sorry. You're obviously a Luminary."

Read: top-tier donor. Most museums compose a creative title for the private class responsible for funding their exhibits, but talking about money in such give-and-take terms is considered gauche. With a starting floor of fifty grand a year, they have to offer more than a nice brass plaque by the front door to keep the cash flowing. *Luminary* projects a sense of power and influence—an inherent superiority.

And they think poor people are the gullible ones.

"No need to apologize." I straighten up anyway, cooling off the distance between us. "I just thought I'd try and get ahead of the game for once. He always pulls some artist out of the vault I've never heard of."

Her eyes widen a touch, suddenly intrigued. Almost everyone loves to get one over on their boss; it's the kind of contrary compulsion that overrides even the strictest training and standards, because chances to push back against the hierarchy are so few and far between.

"I bet you've heard of Russell Key," she says. "Apparently the Institute has a collection of his photos no one's ever seen before."

"Key? Really?" My excitement bleeds through, carefully matching hers. "Where are they even going to put them? Kruger's running this place from top to bottom."

Olivia gestures back over my shoulder. "The director is revamping the entire Contemporary Art wing. Build crew has been in there every night after close for two weeks."

That's where Jillian came from. She can't possibly be—

I have to know.

"You've been an incredible help." I step back from the counter before Olivia can say another word. "Thanks so much."

Walls of curious bodies make the museum an unintentional labyrinth, cutting off the most efficient path. I have to elbow my way back around the café and through another long, narrow hallway that cuts through to Contemporary Art. Signs of construction are everywhere, each exhibit stripped down to skeletons of white paint and empty frames, temporarily abandoned hammers and brushes sitting like props behind sealed glass doors.

Jillian stands in front of the last one of the row, carefully scribbling in a tiny notebook. Her head snaps up at my approach, but she doesn't bother to hide the tools of her trade. Not that it would work anyway; I already know her methods inside and out.

And she's crossed me for the last time.

CHAPTER 5
JILLIAN

Sloane fucking Caffrey.

Three years should have stripped the shine off their smile. It should have undercut their hypnotic voice, riling me like a strip of velvet against bare skin, every word warm and smooth as seventy-year bourbon. They can make ordering coffee sound indecent.

Sloane's hair remains the same, a long, sanguine glory that puts classic romance cover models to shame. Even the color feels like an insult, living proof they're the one percent of the one percent. They always looked suave with their hair tied up and dangerous with it down, like I was a step away from being thrown over their shoulder and carried off.

Today they're dangerous, and it's all I can do to remind myself that Sloane hurt me more than anyone else ever has, and years of vengeance barely salved the wound. Once, I would have welcomed them cornering me in an empty hallway, waiting for some obscene and tempting promise whispered in my ear.

Now, I'm fighting the urge to punch them for daring to be in range.

"What are you doing here?" Sloane snaps.

Real anger clings to the words, and I can't help but savor it. Their coy, friendly façade *can* be scuffed by someone who knows them well enough. "I don't see how that's any of your business. Besides, can't you read my mind?"

My old joke meets its mark; Sloane's mouth tightens into a thin line. "I put that book down a long time ago, jewel. The plot twists verged on sadistic."

Who do they think taught me to be cruel? "Then you can wait for the full release like everyone else. Get in line early enough, and maybe I'll give you an autograph."

"Let me put this another way." One long stride closes the gap between us. Sloane towers over me up close; my tallest heels grant the grace of five foot six, but the slight tilt of their leather Scardinos puts them at six foot three. "If you're planning to steal Russell Key's photos, they're spoken for. Take a nice tourist shot with the Cloud Gate outside and go home."

They're after Key's collection too? You're kidding me.

"Is it really stealing?" I whisper, trying to keep my voice even. If Sloane senses even a hint of weakness, they'll rip it out with their teeth. "These pictures belong to the Key family. His son asked me to recover what they're owed. Plain and simple."

"Suddenly you care about provenance?" Sloane scoffs. "Then I'm sure this recovery is a show of generosity. Pro bono."

A needle of irritation slips under my skin, seeking nerve. "My finder's fee is none of your concern. The Keys want their photos back in the proper hands."

"Maybe last year when Russell's wife was alive," they say. "His son is just going to hawk it for cash."

Their confidence veers on brazen; I can't wait to snuff it out. "And how would you know that, exactly?"

"I watched a few documentaries he was in during the flight here. Equal parts seedy and pathetic. Definitely the kind of man who would sell off his father's finest work for fifty cents on the dollar."

Of course Sloane would think a stack of ego-laden erotica qualifies as Key's finest work; they only have one priority, and it's self-satisfaction. "You're such a cynic."

They smirk. "And you're a mark."

The needle working under my skin explodes into shrapnel, blown apart by a burst of rage. Sloane told me more than once I was their only equal, and hasn't our little competition proved I finally pulled ahead? I'm no one's con and no one's victim. "That isn't true. Take it back."

"I won't. There's such a soft, faithful heart under all that ice." Sloane draws a line in the air, a scarce inch from the bust of my dress. "I would know. I've seen you melt."

A deep breath clears the haze of anger from my mind. If they're here to steal Key's photos too, I have to protect myself. Falling prey to a thousand barbs is exactly what Sloane wants, exhausting my fortitude before the real fight begins. Giving them control over who asks the questions was my first mistake.

"Who hired you?" I demand.

They don't steal for pleasure. Sloane's bread and butter is backroom deals with the higher echelons of the world, then passing the profits into the hands of people who actually need the money. Such generosity would be attractive, if their attitude wasn't so insufferable—self-proclaimed Robin

Hoods rarely deserve the title. "Let me guess. Zouch called you back to his lap to be a good dog again."

Green eyes narrow. "Woof."

How predictable. "I can't believe you keep working for that relic. He's one step away from a Bond villain, and twice as creepy."

"Every British noble is creepy. It's 2023 and they're still buying into the feudal contract." Sloane smiles, a bright and shining lure. "But I consider it my civic duty to redistribute their ill-gotten gains."

"The living embodiment of charity." I flick a nail against the central button of their jacket. "And yet here you are, flaunting a bespoke Ermenegildo Zegna in public. What's that run again—twenty thousand before tailoring?"

They raise a brow. "Clothes are part of the image, Jill. You know that. We can't scam them if we don't look like them."

"There's no *we*," I say, trying to blithely push them back. It doesn't work; Sloane fills out their suit with solid muscle. As much as they frustrate me, the look isn't a surface-level affectation; Sloane plays for keeps. "Just stay out of my way, Caff."

"Right. You're wearing that eyesore of a hat because of this week's Instagram influencer, not because it blocks eighty percent of camera angles and comes in a fetching heliotrope. Human eyes are shit at discerning blues and violets, so the colors filter right out. Terrible weakness."

"You're impossible," I mutter.

"And you're unbearable." Sloane's gaze lingers, a slow scan from head to toe. "How much would it cost to stop you from squatting on my target? I have more cash than Key's offshoot could ever fit in his piggy bank."

Why did I ever believe they respected me? The

implication alone is insulting. "Even you should know better than to try and buy me out."

Sloane laughs, and I curse the low, sultry sound for sending a matched heat between my thighs. "Funny. Last I checked, money is the only thing that's ever mattered to you."

Just like that, the heat boils over, rushing through my blood like venom. They don't have the first idea what it means for your life to hang in the balance over a single dollar, the lint-ridden collection of change in a bowl. Scrounging, scraping, *begging*. Praying for luck to strike, only to find out the world reserves good fortune for people with the right last name. A handful of social factors helped me survive to eighteen; smart white girls are valuable grist for charity, permitting the powers-that-be to claim affirmative action really works, then pretending there isn't a penny to spare for marginalized women clinging to life by a thread.

Would Sloane have suffered worse in my position? Undoubtedly. But they were born near the front of the line, the only child of liberal parents with a crushing monopoly on the California pharmaceutical industry. "Rich" is an understatement when your stock portfolio outclasses the GDP of entire countries.

But I won't let them see my anger. Sloane lost the right to knowing when I give a damn a long time ago.

"What's your point?" I ask. "Nothing's stopping me from donating this fee to the first person I pass on the street."

"You could. But you won't." They're so *sure,* it sets my teeth on edge. "Part of you is always waiting for that rainy day when you need every last cent stuffed under your mattress. No one else gets a piece of that escape."

A mattress? Please. I designed my own vault from scratch, engineering out the weaknesses of every private storage unit on the market. A nuclear bomb wouldn't even make the door shake. "This argument is pointless."

Sloane acquiesces with a shrug. "Clearly."

Yet a glaring problem remains. They've managed to sabotage some of my most complicated thefts from more than a continent away, using a chain of connections and bribes to reach me without lifting a finger. The damage Sloane can do in person is outsized, especially when they throw the weight of their reputation around with various authoritative bodies. I could crack the Institute's repository tonight and be done with it, but they would ensure half the art world was hunting me before I walked out the door. Even the best only have to stumble once to get caught.

I need time for a smokescreen. The sort of gamble that appeals to their sense of theater, drawing everyone's attention until I'm good and gone. If Sloane is left holding the bag and has to explain themself, so much the better.

"Since we're going after the same target, it seems like it would be in our best interest to lay some ground rules," I say.

Amusement sharpens their eyes, giving Sloane a leonine edge. "I thought there was no 'we' to speak of."

Pulling off a perfect heist is irrelevant if I end up in prison for strangling them in public. I have to remember that. "Well, you're a social animal. If I leave you alone for too long, it looks like neglect."

I expect a mocking chuckle, but for a second, their face is unreadable. Sloane keeps a mask on hand for every occasion; seeing them draw a blank is unsettling. Then they blink and summon a perfect smile, shifting back into comfortable camouflage.

"There's only one rule, jewel: no cops." Any sense of humor is gone; I've never heard Sloane's voice freeze on impact. "If you can manage to restrain yourself."

An accusation layers their tone, but I can't pinpoint the source. I've never sicced the police on anybody, not once. Even with Sloane, I wouldn't dare. I want them curled up in a corner licking emotional and financial wounds, not shot to death. Trite as it may be, I do believe in honor among thieves, and tossing jackbooted goons into the mix would desecrate everything I've worked for.

"That's all you're asking for?" I expected them to throw out more bait, verging on the ridiculous: taking the photos blindfolded, leaving behind a calling card, whatever catches their whim. "Because if that's the only safeguard, I can do anything to you."

"A good threat requires specificity," Sloane chides. "'Anything' could be ending up naked with the Byzantine emperors in the East wing or getting locked in a real sarcophagus. Unless you'd rather run my baby pictures on repeat through Film & Media. My parents had terrible taste in toddler fashion, but it doesn't really get the blood pumping."

For fuck's sake. I didn't need to give them yet another avenue to tease me. "You wish I'd give you that much attention."

"I've had the brunt of your *attention* for long enough." Sloane takes a step back, openly dismissive. "No cops. Anything else goes. Whoever gets Key's photos first wins."

Which begs one more question: "What's the prize?"

"That would presume I need anything from you, Jillian. And I don't." Sloane using my full name should feel like a victory, but my heart clenches instead, like someone slipped a knife between fragile chambers and decided to twist. "If by some stroke of luck you win, demand anything you like."

The blade slips out as they turn around, but a warm, bloody pulse lingers under my skin even as Sloane falls out of sight. Hundreds of people are milling around the Institute at this hour, but this particular hallway keeps a sterile silence, white and obliterating as a hospital.

I hate that being around Sloane still feels like standing in the sun when I've always preferred the shadows. With the right words, they can turn me against my own best interests, and I'll plead for the privilege. I hate that I ever let my guard down around them, when they made it clear exactly who they are and what they value from the start. I let myself believe I was the exception, until it was too late.

But first and foremost, I hate that—

Well, all of this happened because we had sex once.

CHAPTER 6

SLOANE

W
e had sex twice.

I try not to repeat mistakes, but Jillian worked her way into my heart like a surgeon, scalpel so fine I forgot about the pain. Our flirtation was a years-long affair, starting months after the first time I heard her name. Despite the secrecy inherent to this profession, people can't help but talk, especially when two very different thieves are on the rise. A joint ascension almost looked planned as we mastered the trade in sister cities: stealing paintings in New York City and Nassau, sculptures displayed throughout Barcelona and Athens, priceless books decorating the vaults of Berlin and Hanoi.

She charmed me by making the first move. After enduring thirty-six hours awake to beat an ivory smuggler at his own game, the last thing I expected was to come back to my hotel and find a silver Fabergé pen-knife on the pillow, its hilt wrapped in an emerald-eyed snake—my favorite animal. The note beside her gift was written impeccably, every letter clean and sharp: *Nice to meet you, Sloane.*

Back when Jillian referred to me by first name.

In return for her generosity, I sussed out a basement she had converted into a surveillance nest next to the Riksbank in Stockholm and left behind Rembrandt's smallest self-portrait, a mere fifteen centimeters. Jillian broke onto the scene by stealing his newly-recovered *The Storm on the Sea of Galilee*, so it seemed fitting. Purloining the portrait from the National Museum four blocks away was remarkably easy; I suspect the Swedes haven't changed their security system since the first theft in 2000.

We gifted each other nearly a million dollars in art before I ever saw her face. Our paths finally intersected here—in Chicago—when I had a layover on the way to London. Zouch wanted me to steal an antique hunting rifle from Prince Andrew's cousin, but two delays on my red-eye meant spending the night in O'Hare. The entire terminal was empty; my fellow passengers had either accepted a rebooking or decided to find a few hours of sleep in a proper bed. Jillian getting caught in the scheduling crossfire felt like fate.

I knew it was her the second she touched me, a light brush over one shoulder. I had claimed a sorrowful gray couch near my boarding gate, and no one else could walk so quietly without catching my ear.

Even now, I don't know where Jillian was flying that night. I only remember spending three halcyon hours talking with her and the moment when teasing one another became spilling our most well-guarded secrets. Who else could understand? I'd never met anyone else with the same intersection of ambition and skill, and it seemed she felt the same.

Six months later, we had our first kiss outside a gallery in

Monaco. Half a year after that, I took her to bed in Paris, taking advantage of a twelve hour eclipse in our schedules.

Yet somehow, giving Jillian exactly what she asked for destroyed everything.

Less than a week later, she lashed out, paying someone to walk off with a suitcase full of sketches I'd recovered from one of Gurlitt's infamous troves. No one else on earth knows my tagging system for travel except for Jillian, although I've changed it twice now to try and muddy her sabotage. She knows my patterns too well, and there's only so many alterations I can make while still keeping my work secure from everyone else.

Walking away from her should have been a simple, logical equation. Yet even after three years of hell, leaving the Contemporary Art wing without saying goodbye felt tantamount to betrayal. If not for the fact that I actually have an appointment with Director Woodward, I might have—

Locked her in the elevator? Kissed her? Who's to say? If I believed in any kind of divine figure, I might ask, but the silence in my own mind is the only consultant on tap.

Clayton Woodward is, as the guard put it, king of the castle. His office looks out over a massive terrace of Richard Hunt's sculptures, showcasing beautiful bronzes like *Scholar's Rock* to the public, mind-bending metallic arms and spiraling petals reaching out toward the Chicago skyline, glistening in every beam of sun. I'm a fan of Hunt's work— he's been in the business for sixty years, and was one of the first Black sculptors to have his pieces displayed across the United States—but my favorite piece of his, *Hero Construction*, is inside and two stories down. I make a mental note to visit it and tap the bell next to Woodward's door.

The blue circle lights up, a miniscule camera above displaying my face to a connected feed. In this case, I don't mind; establishing my presence during legitimate hours is part of the con. A gentle chime rings before the lock clicks, and the door slides silently into its housing to let me in.

Despite the cool minimalist exterior, the director's office is a sprawling ode to the love of art, prints and small sculpture recreations fighting for every inch of space in a room paneled with rustic heart pine, giving the air of a hunting lodge where his quarries were found in a particularly chaotic preserve. A copy of Rodin's *Eve* guards Woodward's nameplate, her accompanying *Adam* slumped in defeat beside the director's pens.

The man himself looks like the Greeks carved his shoulders, broad and stately against the ruddy leather of an antique chair. He's forty years out from a brief college football career, but the solid presence remains, black hair buzzed down an inch from the scalp and a short, impeccably trimmed beard framing his warm brown face from chin to jaw in tight, well-oiled curls. When Woodward stands, we're of a height, and he offers me his hand in tandem with a smile.

"Sloane Caffrey, I presume." His handshake is firm but not aggressive, which I appreciate. Some men can't help themselves, depending on how they read me. "Welcome to the Art Institute."

I return his smile. "I've actually been here quite a few times, Director. This is one of the best museums in the world."

"Clayton's fine. And thank you, I'm doing my best to keep it that way." Rather than sitting back down, he leans back against his desk. "Taking over for Rondeaux has had some interesting challenges."

'Rondeaux' and not 'Jason'. His bad blood with the previous director might as well be spilled on the floor in front of me. "You're coming up on twelve months in the seat, aren't you?"

Clayton nods. "You pay attention. Unfortunately, a lot of people who sing about supporting the arts lose their voice when it's time to cash the checks."

He's blunt, which I respect. I positioned myself as a generous investor on the phone to his secretary, but plenty of flighty millionaires make claims about charitably donating their fortunes, only to back out at the last second. The thought of their bank accounts shrinking by a digit is too much to bear, even if next year's investments will double what they own.

"I'd like to think my reputation precedes itself," I say, "but if you want references, pick a city and I'll get someone on the line."

His laugh is a warm, rolling bass. "No, you're right. It's an impressive accomplishment, building a fortune from scratch after your family loses everything."

They didn't lose anything. I cut it out from under them to try and stem the flow of countless wounds they inflicted on other people: patients turned victims. Caffrey Chemical took a middling pharmacy chain and spent the next two decades rerouting their money into legal opioid production. Business —and addiction—boomed.

I remember the first time I realized the numbers my father discussed over dinner weren't profits but actual human beings, condensed down into convenient data: doses, relapses, deaths. At ten years old, I could only sit and listen. By fourteen, I'd acquired my parents' private passwords. By sixteen, I had a plan and the names of everyone on the executive board.

Fifteen years later, they still haven't recovered, and if I have my way, they never will. A class action lawsuit in the billions may have helped grieving families in need, but the buried are still buried. Demolishing my inheritance from the ground up can't be called justice; that money was never mine to begin with.

"Art is far less stressful than medicine," is what I say aloud, holding my smile in place. "Which is why I'm excited to talk. A little bird told me about your surprise exhibition."

Clayton's dark brows knit together. "So much for keeping secrets. Key's notoriety seems to have survived his passing."

"That's what you're banking on, isn't it?" I ask. "Everyone wants a taste when fame is on the table. The Institute will be drowning in donations soon enough."

Brown eyes lock on mine, hard and serious. "Because we need them. My... predecessor acquired those photos, but he left a mess in his wake. If I had my way, the Institute wouldn't have to shock and awe the public into buying tickets."

And the pressure on Clayton is twofold. Like his sculptor contemporary outside, he's the first Black director since the Institute's founding in the 1800s, coming out of a decade where arts funding has been slashed from the federal level at every opportunity. The city itself isn't any better—Chicago has a vested interest in directing their coffers towards the pockets of police and pork barrel legislation, even when the city is starved for new infrastructure, and free programs for children close their doors every day.

"I can't imagine I'm the only person to come up here to try and get a sneak peek at the Key pictures." When Clayton gives me a knowing look, I continue: "What I want to know is how much they're putting on the table. I can be competitive."

He turns to his desk and grabs a manila folder stuffed with papers before idly waving it in my direction. "Enough to hold an auction, if I could risk the hit to the Institute's reputation. But if a single reporter finds out I'm restricting access to the rich and famous, I'll be a mockery in the *Tribune* by sunup. So we're having a gala instead. Unrelated, of course."

Smart. Gathering every would-be donor in the same place means they'll see one another, sparking enough old grudges to drive up the price for the sheer pleasure of peacocking in front of their rivals. The Institute can give a glimpse to whoever wins and open the doors to the public the next day. No one will be the wiser.

I smile. "Are tickets still on sale?"

"Our Platinum Luminary package includes two seats at every private event." Translation: fifty thousand dollars a plate. "But memberships are a drop in the bucket, and I think we both know that."

If nothing else, the gala might be my ticket to an alibi. "Forget an early preview. If I wanted my name on a plaque sponsoring the exhibit, how much would it run? Just the number. You don't have to coddle my ego."

Clayton frowns. "Five million. And you would still have competition."

The museum must be mired in debt. My guess was around half that amount—no wonder the previous director was ousted. "And there's nothing I can do to pull ahead of the pack?"

For a second, he doesn't answer. Clayton's gaze turns analytical, taking in everything from the thread count of my suit to the hand-stitching along the soles of each shoe. Signals of quality, no expense spared. People want to believe that such things reflect on morals, on loyalty, as if a fine enough exterior is obligated to reflect the same within. The world is easier to accept when we walk in line with prosperity gospel, that being good is just a matter of making enough money, regardless of what's given up along the way.

"That depends," Clayton says. "Do you happen to be single?"

I haven't been with anyone since Jillian. Seducing on the job is straightforward, but all I really offer is an illusion, stringing along enough promises until I have what I need. There's no feeling in it, just a Rolodex of lines and lingering touches most people fall for, hoping they've finally found a soulmate.

Clayton's question is interesting, though, because gut instinct tells me I'm not his type. "At the moment, yes. Why?"

"Because I have an inkling that you and my daughter would get along quite well." He gestures to the only framed photo on his desk, where Clayton stands next to an ecstatic young woman posing with her Alpha Kappa Alpha stole. "Ella graduated from Yale like yourself. She just finished her master's in Art History."

I'd rather crawl over broken glass than endure the Ivy League again, but most white collar cabals expect certain letters after your name before they treat you like a fully realized person. Robbing the relics from their so-called secret societies was amusing, at least. "We'd have a lot to talk about, then. I specialized in painting and printmaking."

In other words—forgery.

"So I heard. My daughter is remarkably busy, and tells me she has trouble finding... like minds." Clayton clears his throat, couching his words with care. "I'm not just looking for an investment in this museum, but in a legacy. I'd much rather contract with a friend of the family than someone who pulls their portfolio the second financial winds change."

I have to give the director credit. He knows enough about

my public image that I imagine this was part of his gambit from the start, waiting to find out what I wanted before offering up a very different trade. A lot of the doors Rondeaux held open have probably been slammed shut in Clayton's face; he needs different paths of access, and I look like new money in need of a cause.

"I'd love to meet her." From the picture, I wager Ella is halfway through her twenties. The same ambitious warmth draped over Clayton like a cloak surrounds her too, driven to win no matter the cost. I'm familiar with the feeling. "Does she enjoy photography?"

"With a little less showmanship than Key's work, but yes." Clayton chuckles. "If you two hit it off, I wouldn't mind giving you a personal preview."

He's just made my day. "If she's free tonight, I have reservations on tap at the Berkshire Room."

In my opinion, the six hundred dollar whiskey isn't worth it, but Clayton lets out a quiet hum of approval. "Wonderful. Can I give Ella your number?"

I bring out my phone, swiping to an app with a QR code displayed onscreen. "This has everything. I bought in on a startup in San Francisco that's trying to turn everyone's business cards digital."

He scans it using his own cell without a second's hesitation. The website it opens has root-level malware built in, enough for me to hijack Clayton's SIM card and do whatever I like with the information inside. Anyone can accomplish this in minutes. The fact that every restaurant and street vendor is switching over to menus easily subverted with a basic printer and a bit of technical know-how astounds me, but I'm happy to take advantage until security vendors catch on.

"She'll be in touch." Clayton pockets his phone. "And the

gala is on Friday. You can put in your Luminary application in at the front desk, and I'll make sure it's processed ASAP."

Considering what I plan to steal, the Institute is welcome to my donation. "Thank you very much, Clayton."

His eyes find mine, sharp with intent. "Just so we're clear. This arrangement goes both directions. If you disrespect my daughter in any way, I don't care how much money you have. I'll make sure you never set foot in this museum again. Am I understood?"

My plans don't involve hurting anyone. All I need is Ella's attention for a few days. "Absolutely."

Clayton nods decisively, then returns to his storied seat to see me off with a smile.

I'm halfway down the office-side stairs when I spy Jillian heading out the front door. The fact that we're after the same collection is a cosmic joke. But if anything will prove I'm the better half of our equation, it's taking Key's photos out from right under her nose. She won't know what hit her.

Even when she disappears from view, my heart keeps pounding at a thousand miles an hour, hard enough to be distracting.

I need to dunk my head in some cold water. If I don't cool down, I'm going to start screwing up.

CHAPTER 7
JILLIAN

T he Art Institute of Chicago is more than a museum. It's essentially a campus claiming an entire section of downtown, sprawling out to their curator's college across the street and throughout the span of Millennium Park for several blocks, providing tourists and students with the essentials for a day's entertainment. Food trucks have their own special lanes between every stretch of grass, with decorative bridges nearby allowing pedestrians to cross over the streets unscathed. Anyone walking past can see their silver reflection on the Cloud Gate or rest their feet on tree-shaded benches; in the middle of the year, the local administration turns on a set of interactive water features, free for children and adults alike to play in at their leisure. During the winter, everything is converted into a massive ice rink.

Thankfully, the weather is holding on the pleasant side of warm, so I secure a seat beside Crown Fountain, where a fifty-foot-tall video screen filled with LEDs dances in a flow of colorful light, the spouts above providing a waterfall for the curious and overheated to dart through whenever they please. I'm well out of the splash radius, but the constant spill of noise rubs against my thoughts like steel wool.

If only it would scour my mind clean, rather than scratching against old scars.

The air is a mix of sun-blooming flowers and sticky sweet sugar, chocolate and fried confections glistening under the sunlight as they're liberated from the spray-painted freezers wedged into every truck. My appetite is entirely absent, yet another void in my body left behind in Sloane's wake.

You're a mark.

Like I suspected, our relationship was a con from the very beginning. We spent so long circling each other back in the day, I couldn't help but make a move, hoping to grab their attention. My first gift was their opening, revealing my weakness—that I wanted a partner in the game. I've refused offers for collaborations and group heists a hundred times over my career, because trusting anyone I had something in common with could only be self-sabotage. Sloane was supposed to be the exception.

I believed it when they left a Rembrandt beside my laptop, answering the note I'd sent with one of their own: *It's nice to meet you too. I hope this humble gift is to your taste.*

Humble. God, as if anything about them is humble. Back then, I devoured Sloane's deference, starved for a real connection. Every successful theft attracted attention, but not the kind I wanted. Our gray little world is rife with disbelief, jealousy, and hostility, because dependence is for people who get scammed, and anyone caught hanging on deserves exactly what they get. After cutting ties from my family, the solitude felt like a blessing—but too much of a good thing sours in time.

My phone vibrates with a text. I keep a few numbers

available for forwarding purposes; maintaining burners twenty-four seven is a waste of both time and money. But I'm not expecting any messages, so I frown and check the screen.

Up to anything fun, Jillian?

Ah, Elias. Of course.

Elias Denning is a mid-tier fence, using several carefully acquired citizenships to move goods around western Europe. I don't sell through him often, but we've known each other long enough to get coffee when I happen to be in town. This line of work doesn't leave much space to vent; honesty with anyone not on the take risks prosecution.

Business as usual, I text back. *I'm not in your part of the world at the moment.*

He texts back a line of eye emoji, which I ignore. Too much is on my mind to bother sating his curiosity.

"Colin, where did the money go?" a girl by the fountain demands, catching my attention. "You were supposed to hold onto it."

She's fifteen, maybe, but carries herself with the mantle of an older sister condemned to early adulthood. The boy with her can't be more than seven, wearing a striped shirt and basketball shorts soaked through from the fountain. His posture is one of defeat, shoulders hunched in, hands clenched into round, shaking fists.

"Dunno," he mutters. "I can't find it."

"Mom should have just given the cash to me. How does she expect you to be responsible when you're just—" Real anger surfaces in her eyes, dark and sharp as flint, but she tamps it back down with a sniffle. Both of them are trying not to cry. "We have to get groceries before going home."

It's a weekday afternoon. Both of them should be in school, but the purse around the girl's shoulder speaks to other responsibilities. Coming to Millennium Park is free, one of the few places in the city where cops won't hound the young and dispossessed. Perfect for letting a boy like Colin burn off anxious energy and somewhere for her to set the burden of responsibility aside for just a little while. A couple hours of normalcy, of being like everyone else.

I'm an only child, but fights with my mother held a similar edge, the desperate assignment of blame. The notion of *if you weren't here, I wouldn't have to deal with this*, like being born is a choice we check off on the way out of the womb. Having children is never a solution to misery; if anything, they're bound to be targets for the same suffering their parents were trying to escape.

The bills in my handbag start at fifty and go up from there, but I pull out several and fold them tight. It will look like less than it is, a more acceptable gift from a stranger. I abandon the bench, keeping my approach casual. The girl doesn't even notice me until the shadow of my hat falls over her eyes.

"I'm sorry if we were being loud," she starts by reflex, tensing for an accusation of truancy. "We were just leaving."

"Then you should get some water and sunscreen from the corner store," I say, holding out the cash between two fingers. "Both of you are getting pink around the cheeks."

A wholly familiar disdain enters her eyes, there and gone in a split second. To *need* charity, faced with no other option but to starve, damages more than pride. It eats at who you are like acid, narrowing down the possibilities of who you can become. I know the sting of waiting for the other shoe to drop or performing a song and dance to keep such generosity directed your way, but in this case, there's no strings attached.

Sloane never asked anything of me in return when we were together either. Not a single penny or favor.

Why can't I stop thinking about them?

"You're a nice lady," Colin mumbles, then glances at his sister for confirmation. "Isn't she a nice lady?"

"Yeah. Of course." She takes the money from me and uncrinkles the bills before her eyes flare wide. "This is—"

"Use the rest for a rainy day," I gently interrupt. "*Your* rainy day. Not your mother's."

The girl swallows hard before stuffing the money deep into her purse, safe from anyone else's hands. "Thank you."

She tugs her brother away before he can start asking questions, making a beeline for the CVS on Michigan and Lake. As they fall out of view, an aftershock of surprise stops me still.

I've never done anything like that before. I'm not sure what possessed me.

Much as I loathe to admit it, Sloane is right about my miserly habits. At first, my caution was born from dire necessity, but as stashed change turned to hundreds—thousands, millions—the need to keep it to myself was forged out of utterly illogical fear. One bad financial forecast can provoke a nigh-apocalyptic chain of events in my mind, where every last dollar is spoken for, needed to keep my life from falling apart.

It was true for long enough. Memory means more than reality sometimes.

I didn't even have to become a thief. A path to a better life opened up when I was fourteen, idly playing in the high school chess club because that classroom had air conditioning and the rotting trailer I grew up in didn't. Matches were boring because I always won, until the teacher sponsoring the club asked me to try out at a local tournament. I won there just as easily, and people started paying attention. The next competition came with prize money, and suddenly, my parents cared too.

Despite rating deep in the 2000s and being offered a full scholarship to Columbia, I detest chess. The rules are the same every time, with a limited amount of legal moves and equations. As a sport, it's slow and oddly grueling, and being tied to a little board and its pieces for hours a day because no other opportunities to eat properly or buy new clothes ever presented themselves left me livid.

Then, my coach offered to take me on a trip to London.

The British Museum is one of the world's largest monuments to theft and exploitation, although they aggressively polish away accusations of the latter and justify the former. As a teenager, I didn't understand the full context, but I did see the Isle of Lewis chess set locked behind glass, and as a droll curator explained every detail—eight hundred years old, carved from walrus ivory by meticulous hands in Trondheim—I wanted nothing more than to put my hands on the pieces.

Stealing wasn't even the point, at first. I craved *access*, the ability to open doors without someone else doing the deed for me. So at three in the morning, with my guardian asleep in our chilly hotel, I walked back to the museum, stepped between the angles of the cameras I observed earlier, and used a keycard one of the docents had kindly left unattended at his post to enter the chess exhibit.

Very few pieces of art have pressure sensors or any sort of alarm. Social trust protects the majority, presuming no one will be bold enough to break open a glass case in public and run past security. Half of the British Museum's galleries don't even have lockable doors, so it took little more than time and a pair of gloves to hold the Lewis pieces in my hands, touching centuries-old majesty without a single person's permission. After playing a few theoretical games on the floor, I returned the little figures to their cage, closed it, and went back to the hotel.

As soon as we returned to the States, I quit the chess team and took every remaining cent of my winnings before leaving home. Being a few months shy of eighteen caused a few complications, but I wasn't troubled. London proved I could have anything I wanted, so long as I figured out the parameters of a building. The same is true of art, fame, and people.

But only one museum is important now. I look back over my shoulder at the Art Institute, its broad, rising planes of glass and concrete. Impenetrable from the outside, or so it seems. In order to find out, I need the blueprints.

Thankfully, the Chicago Architecture Center is only a ten minute walk away. The organization keeps dozens of city designs in trust, usually loaned to builders and engineers trying to preserve century-old exteriors in conjunction with modern amenities. Most tourists never see them, too distracted by the miniature models and 3D projections of theoretical future cities, but I know exactly where to go.

"Hi." I take off my sunglasses and smile at the woman standing behind the front desk. "I'm looking for the blueprint archive. Late 19th century."

"Oh, of course." The delight of conspiracy lines her eyes; I'm sure she's used to a hundred questions a day about the Great Fire rather than anything of substance. "I'll show you to that section. We have a reading room available upstairs. Nothing can leave the building, but feel free to scan whatever you like."

Away from the spectacle of brightly lit replicas, a simple room full of staid drawers holds my prize. They're made from the light, waxy wood of countless school desks from the fifties with simple brass keyhole locks, but the receptionist leaves me alone absent fear. The top drawers slide open, intended for public consumption, because everything inside references buildings that no longer stand.

Nonetheless, they make a good cover. A single camera in the ceiling peers down at me, so I pull the first 19th century drawer open with one hand and start idly flicking through the blueprints. Angling two lockpicks with my other hand is a bit of a pain, but I've always had flexible fingers, and a few simple tumblers are no challenge. When the second drawer clicks open, I run my thumb over the tabs, seeking the texture of my chosen year: 1877, 1878, 1879—

There.

I slip a blueprint from the top drawer at the same time, a suitable veil for the one from the Institute. Everything slides closed with one clean push, and I'm pleased to discover the Center's reading room has no survelliance to speak of. My quiet dissection of the Institute's contemporary wing and its surrounding accessways goes unremarked, so after a solid hour of notes, I return both aging sheets to their dusty home.

I'll do the rest at the hotel. Between the constant crush of tourists and Sloane, a bit of alone time will set my head straight.

CHAPTER 8
SLOANE

The indoor pool at the Peninsula is exactly to my taste.

A lot of hotels—even the five-star ones—offer tepid fare: little basins shaped into logos or animals not more than three feet deep, designed to attract pictures for social media rather than athletic activity. Here, three Olympic lanes lined with electric blue tile stretch from one arm of the building to the other, providing nearly two hundred feet of crisp, cool water, and a full view of the Chicago skyline through floor-to-ceiling windows.

I have the entire chamber to myself, chasing the abstract art pieces at each end of the lane with every lap. Twenty gets my heart moving, forty floods every muscle with adrenaline's acid sting, but by sixty, I've forgotten everything but the water flowing over my body, a simple rhythm of breathe, kick, push.

At least, that was the intention.

Jillian might as well be lounging on one of the plush seats by the water's edge for the way she keeps catching my eye, a mirage lingering right above the surface. Three years. I thought I remembered what it was like to be in her presence, the inescapable magnetism drawing me into her orbit, but there's no comparison to the real thing. Except she's not a star, some beautiful guiding light. She's a black hole, taking anything I have to offer with cold, careless gravity and refusing to spit a damn thing back out.

I know desire when I see it. Even her show-off pair of sunglasses—Versace Medusas, truly on the nose—can't hide the way Jillian reacts whenever I'm close. The hunger isn't gone, merely escorted by hate, held on a choke chain to keep it from wandering too far. I always thought there was more than lust between us, though. A quick fuck with the right person is fun, but why would I settle for that, knowing everything else we've left on the table?

She doesn't want a partner. Her world is self-contained and complete, save for the occasional amusement she darts out to devour. Consumptive, claiming, as if Jillian ate some part of me and I can't steal it back. When a scar seals over a wound, it's a stopgap, jagged tissue trying to conceal what's been lost, but in truth, it sends a signal to everyone else, telling them you've never healed clean. That she can walk around untouched, ruining me on a whim, burns more than the chlorine clawing at my lungs.

Breaking the surface brings a measure of relief, but I lost count of my laps somewhere around the eighty mark. I wade back to the shallows, breathing so hard I can't hear anything but the cacophony of noise carrying from my heart. Stripping off my goggles clears the watercolor blur from my vision, but the world remains unsteady.

We crossed paths in Rio de Janeiro once—after Monaco, before Paris. I had a few spare hours after waylaying a smuggler trying to sell a piece from the old Chácara do Céu heist. Returning a piece to a museum is rare for me, but the original thieves held dozens of people hostage at gunpoint, which is against my personal rules. I already have enough blood on my hands by proxy. So I put *Toros* back in its rightful place, passed the government's grateful fee to a few friends of the Awá, and decided to spend the rest of the evening by the ocean.

Jillian walked down the sand as I was coming out of the water and set up shop on my solitary towel stretched out along the beach. It was four in the morning, but my flight wasn't until seven, so she brought coffee and crepes from one of the late-night feiras for the two of us to share. I didn't ask how she found me, just like she never asked how I found her; it was one of the unspoken rules of our rendezvous, guarding each other's mystique like a ritual.

A wayward Matisse brought her to Brazil, but we didn't discuss the details. I was looking for any excuse to kiss her again when Jillian remarked on how much she enjoyed being alone. Even the powdered sugar lacing every layer of the crepes couldn't stop bitterness from filling my mouth, although I had no room to judge. She was always open about her solitude and how it released her from haunting obligations at a young age. Jillian wanted to move through the world, frictionless, without anything holding her back.

What's it like being by yourself all the time? I asked, as if I wasn't the same, like I had anything to hold onto but our chain of happy accidents.

Her laugh was bright, outshining the stars. *I don't think I could survive if I wasn't.*

I taste the same bitterness now. Here I am, alone, because of her.

"You're kidding," an irritated voice carries through the

door to the pool, warped by layers of glass. "There's enough room for a hundred people in there."

"A guest made a special request from management," Martina—the attendant who let me in—answers. "I'm sorry, miss, but if you come back in an hour, the pool will be available."

I don't have another hour in me. Better to save Martina some misery.

After taking off my cap to let my hair back down and wrapping a towel around my hips, I open the door, ready to break the tension with a smile—or maybe a little flexing—only to lock gazes with Jillian. Every drop of water on my body turns to ice.

"*You?*" Amber eyes narrow in sudden, scintillating entrapment. "Of course it's you. Who else reserves a hotel-sized pool completely to themself?"

Only sheer willpower stops me from rolling my eyes. I wanted privacy; this wasn't an exercise in narcissism. "Have you ever considered I don't let the majority of people see me nearly naked? I'm not welcome in most locker rooms."

Which is why I'm always in suits, blazers, polos. Formal layers, carefully constructed. Society trusts the masculine more than the feminine, so it's how I dress, even though I'm neither. I rely too much on appearances to risk getting undercut by casual misogyny. Plenty of cis women in the trade use an expectation of weakness to their advantage, but one wrong assumption about what I "really" am is violence waiting to happen.

Jillian's anger stops short, withering in the face of surprise. "Fair enough."

She must have come upstairs to swim too. Love of the water is one of the few hobbies we have in common beyond grand larceny. I started diving before puberty reared its ugly head because my parents owned a facility situated away from the rest of the house, and it was as much distance as I could get from them until I was old enough to drive. Jillian told me once that public pools were her only savior during summers in Desert Hills, where the temperature never fell below triple digits.

Swimming is safe, distant. Nobody touches you unless you're already intimate.

But that doesn't explain why she's *here*. "You always go to the Langham in Chicago. What changed?"

She frowns. "They're doing construction on several floors. I never stay in a hotel I can't climb out of the hard way."

Understandable—by her standards. Of course, she could be lying, but our reflexive honesty with each other is a hard habit to break. Leaving out information or refusing to answer is one thing, but full-on fabrication is for people who will never know better.

Part of me wants to ask Jillian her room number, and the rest is tempted to change hotels out of sheer spite, but I won't give her the pleasure of running me off, and who knows what she would read into the first question.

"Enjoy the water, Jill," I say, taking my wallet out of my swim bag so I can leave Martina a hefty tip. No one deserves to be cornered by an argument between strangers. "This pool is exactly the way you like it."

She rises to the bait with a huff. "Cold?"

"And empty." I lean down to whisper in her ear, "Just like your bed. Hopefully, the ones on the lower floors suit. I took the penthouse."

Her teeth flash in a sneer, tight and vulpine. "What a shame. Did you think I preferred you on top?"

I laugh, then force myself to walk away. The last thing I

need is remembering how Jillian felt underneath me, nails biting into my back as she gasped for me not to stop, to *never* stop. I took her at her word until we were both exhausted, so wrung out with pleasure I forgot where the boundaries between my body and Jillian's began. Then, we caught our breath and started over again anyway.

So why did it stop? Back then, I would have come to her every night, if she had asked.

The penthouse's luxurious silence now has an oppressive weight. Standing in a hot shower gets the chlorine off my skin but doesn't wash out a single drop of poison from my mind. I'm supposed to be planning the Key heist, and yet I'm half-tempted to run back downstairs and yell at her, demanding an explanation for why she put me through hell.

Not that it matters anymore. Jillian might have shoved me into the first circle, but we've been digging each other deeper ever since. I won't stop until she does, because admitting defeat now would make me twice the fool. We can skate around the ice of treachery together until the world ends if it gets my point across.

My phone buzzes. I brace for a text from Jillian—she knows I have to keep a legitimate number on hand for appearance's sake—but the message is from Ella Woodward.

I've always wanted to go to the Berkshire Room. Is that offer still open?

It's 6:05. I can be back in my suit and down at the bar by seven, which gives me the rest of the night to talk Ella into making me her father's new favorite. If I'm lucky, it might even be an interesting conversation.

Other women besides Jillian exist. Reminding myself of that isn't a bad idea.

CHAPTER 9
JILLIAN

An hour in the pool should have cleared my head, but going through the Institute blueprints is making me dizzy. I had to cleave several scans from my phone together and hijack a wireless printer in one of the Peninsula's staff rooms for a clean copy large enough to roll out across the desk and make notes on. Ensuring every level fit cleanly together is half the battle, and that's before accounting for architecture lost to the ravages of time.

Yet the lines still aren't perfect. The Institute built substantial additions in 1898 and 1901, followed by half a dozen new wings throughout the twentieth century. I layer those in place on top of the original blueprint—there's a roll of translucent drafting paper in my entry kit for a reason—but trying to discover the weak points in a building with two hundred different galleries takes time. The basement-turned-vault is sparsely detailed, although a wide set of attached emergency doors catches my eye.

Safety sells on illusion. Most imposing steel locks can be clipped open with a cheap set of wire cutters from the hardware store, guards everywhere with a weekend's worth of training are shoved into clunky blue uniforms to suggest the intimidating aura—or budget—of police, and even a jewelry store full of diamonds has to meet a series of predictable and exploitable construction codes. Saving lives of those inside is an incidental feature; any insurance adjuster will tell you that policies won't pay out if valuables in the way of disaster were made too difficult to evacuate. Fear of losing out on a claim is probably the only thing keeping the rich from burying their gold like squirrels.

I reach for my water, then flinch at the slick, room temperature glass. The ice melted a while ago, leaving a veil of condensation in its place. A clear drop slips defiantly over my fingertips, the same way I watched finger-wide rivulets traverse Sloane's abs as they came dripping out of the pool.

God, if they hadn't been so shocked by running into me, they would have noticed. I've seen them sans suit before, but the physical, visceral reminder of how much muscle is smoothed out by layers of linen and silk almost made me forget what I was angry about in the first place. If I close my eyes and picture them, my fingers can call up the echo of every inch of skin, the way Sloane gave in when they wanted me.

Past tense, of course. Their disdain for me now is clear, although the comment about how few people have gotten them naked lingers in the back of my mind, grinding like the teeth of a key that refuses to catch.

I thought what we had was special. If Sloane thought the same, then why did they—

Our relationship, if such a farce deserves the name, ended the same way it began: with a note on a pillow. Ten little words, constructed to ruin me.

Christ. I need a drink.

I also need to get this heist off the ground before Sloane waltzes into the Institute and ruins my best-laid plans.

Not that my plans involve getting laid. Maybe I should change that, if only as another way to de-Caff my life. If they manage to distract me from walking off with Key's photos, I'll never live it down.

After quiet consideration, I make a deal with myself to work on this for another hour before taking a break at the Z Lounge. The Peninsula maintains a pretty glass balcony with a full bar at the top of the hotel, providing guests with custom cocktails and imported spirits until one in the morning. With the urge to blank my memory with a glass of Macallan becoming more insistent, I pick up my pencil again and start to sketch.

A vault-side entry would require matching the requisite Institute uniform and getting ahold of their schedule to time an insertion properly. My purse recordings confirmed their outdoor rotations are every twenty-five minutes, with a small gap when perimeter guards descend and do a sweep of the underground floor. That transition is my best bet as a back-up plan, if getting into the Contemporary Art wing directly proves too fraught.

I bring up the museum's public floor plan on my laptop. Out of respect for guests vulnerable to noise and large crowds, they provide a sensory map, which conveniently marks which paths through the Institute are closed. A red line cuts back behind the café through the rooms where Key's photos are supposed to be housed, connected to three different staircases and the elevator I took notes on. The International Modern Art gallery is immediately above, with a point of access through reinforced panes in the roof.

It's also closed for the season. I remember an issue with their "flying carpet" mechanism hitting the news more than a decade ago, where aluminum screens threaded with photovoltaic cells ended up at war with the actual sun, inadvertently dimming the entire gallery rather than adjusting light levels to meet the time of day. Constant but minute fluctuations confused their motion detection sensors and almost damaged a Matisse painting on display due to irregular exposure. Cursory research tells me the system has been replaced twice now, although a long-term closure suggests the weakness persists.

I'll need to climb to the roof and unscrew at least two panels by hand, but it's still the preferable path. The alternatives are dodging guards on the nearby terrace and the floors below or drilling through a solid limestone wall.

Plan A doesn't account for the photos themselves, though. Camera coverage on the contemporary side was minimal, which means they can't be relying on a matrix of surveillance to subdue would-be thieves. Nothing I saw under construction implied wire work or permanent frames, so the housing for Key's collection must be mobile. Fire and waterproofing are a given, and every room in a museum is already filtered to maintain the right temperature and humidity. Other factors I have to guess at: explosive-resistant casings, digitized locks tied to a fob, a granite base to prevent drilling in entry from below.

But this is supposed to be new. Rumors of 'impossible' safes and display cases run rampant amongst the thieving crowd, although the majority are million-dollar boondoggles stacking familiar layers of protection over one another. The hope is that someone skilled at cracking mechanical safety features won't have the same knack for subverting biometric codes or the right tools on hand to handle tempered glass compounded with steel and stone. Annoy a would-be thief enough, and they won't bother when so many other easy targets are waiting out in the open. The strategy is sound: most professionals care more about profit and safety than showing off to everyone else.

What can I say? I'm an overachiever.

Unfortunately, lack of context means I need to get back inside the museum and find one of the photo cases to get an idea of what I'm working with. It will be more time spent, but I can double up on plotting my route in through the roof and plant that camera; no one's good enough to skip a practice run. If I happen to gather information on the vault security to buffer my plan B, so much the better.

I've earned that drink.

After locking everything back in my luggage—the FBI has nothing on a nosy maid in the right place at the right time—I change into a midi dress styled with a monochrome gradient, dripping black over white along bosom to hem. Paired in tandem with some Manolo Blahniks, the look is expensive enough to pass with the Z Lounge crowd, and good camouflage means less attention.

At this hour, most patrons are seeking digestifs after a tightly wound meal somewhere on Michigan Street or a drink to numb broken promises, missed dates, anniversaries. The bartender is young but efficient, catching my eye on entry before gesturing to an empty corner seat. It's up at the counter, but I like having my back to the wall, even if that wall is a barricade of spotless glass, so I claim the chair and wait for him to finish a tasting tray, sampling heavy from Japanese whisky.

"Good evening, ma'am." He keeps his voice carefully low; a faint crack at the bottom of one syllable speaks to late-in-life testosterone. I'm surprised the Peninsula lets him get away with the tattoos peeking out of rolled sleeves and a stiff white collar, but maybe his manager was convinced the flowers add to the atmosphere. "What can I create for you tonight?"

A canned, airless introduction. No one with money *drinks* anymore—it's mixology and hand-crafted innovation, top to bottom. "Do you have Macallan 12 year on hand?"

When he nods, I add, "I'll take a glass then. Room temperature, please."

I mentally double his tip when he doesn't try and upsell me on one of the hotel's branded cocktails, with extra points for not assuming a woman needs water in her scotch. Watching red-spun amber liquor limn the tumbler is a pleasure in and itself, until the spell is broken by a soft voice from my right.

"You have expensive taste."

The culprit is svelte, femme, and secure enough not to hide the subtle signs of slipping past thirty. Blonde hair falls loose around her shoulders in the kind of devil-may-care curls the finest salons charge an obscenity to recreate, but she seems to come by the style naturally. I wager she avoids the sun as a habit to stay so pale, and her eyes are a gelid blue, the same shade trapped in the center of a glacier.

"I have very poor taste, actually," I reply with a faint smile. "When I was twenty, I looked up the priciest liquors in the world so I would be able to brag to other people. But then I actually had a sip—and wouldn't you know it—good as advertised."

She laughs, warm and genuine. If the implication I grew up with very little doesn't make her recoil, I suppose carrying on a conversation is a good enough way to pass the time.

"I can't judge," she notes, "I'm the cheapest date out of all my friends."

"Vodka?" I ask. After a nod, I add, "Grey Goose, probably. Cut with lime to kill the aftertaste."

Surprise rounds her eyes. "Do I have it written on my face or something?"

I could spin a tale about alcohol trends among certain demographics, but the simple fact is I've met enough people to learn common patterns, and a solitary woman patronizing an American bar at this hour rarely falls out of the same societally prescribed lanes of taste. We all like to pretend we're the heroines of our own stories, though, so I say, "Lucky guess."

Her smile is real too, so open despite not having a drop of alcohol in her system yet. "Very lucky. My name's Laurel."

"Jillian." I don't conceal my first name very often—one of the benefits of never being caught. "What are you looking for tonight, Laurel?"

She bites her lip, hesitant and sensitive. "You're blunt, too."

But she likes it, I can tell. It's not hard to believe Laurel would be sensitive in every way, eager to please. Odds are I could have her wet, willing, and whimpering my name inside of ten minutes, easy as pulling cards with two aces already up my sleeve.

Except I don't want a one-night stand. I want someone who knows me to the bone, who can pry me apart with the same ease I do everyone else. If I can't be met blow for blow, then there's no point.

Before Sloane, I made regular trips around the block, but since having them, no offer on the table seems to promise enough. They would laugh at my reflexive chastity—I can't imagine their trousers have stayed zipped for the last three years—but fucking a stranger out of spite for someone else is too cruel by proxy for me to swallow.

"I like people who take what they want," I say out loud,

trying to etch the apology to come in my expression. "But not tonight. I'm sorry."

Laurel accepts the rejection with grace, excusing herself to the opposite end of the counter as my Macallan arrives. It was ready a few minutes ago, but the best bartenders know when not to interrupt. I hand him a couple of bills, deny the change, and take a long sip.

By some mercy, the scotch is perfect.

A small victory, but it emboldens me. For a second, I imagine ripping down Sloane's entire house of cards by handing over a file of evidence to the first fed that would take it, cherry-picked to drop everyone from Interpol to Homeland Security on their head. The fantasy is more than enough, though. I could never hate Sloane more than I hate the cops. No matter the department, scratching the surface reveals fascists of a different stripe.

I'm going to beat Sloane on my own terms.

They won't ever hurt me again. I'll make sure of it.

CHAPTER 10
SLOANE

Ella Woodward arrives at the Berkshire Room five fashionable minutes late.

She's a vision in gold, cutting a fine A-line silhouette in a spread collar dress intent on claiming every passing band of light, the glint of silk reflecting up to a pair of sunburst earrings, each one punctuated with an onyx center. Black, voluminous curls bounce down to bare shoulders, a hair's breadth away from the deep umber of her skin. Amusement flickers through brown eyes as she approaches me, taking in the corner of the bar carved out for VIPs and their cohorts.

"You *did* have reservations," Ella says, sitting down when I gesture to the other side of the booth. "A lot of people try to impress me with the cheap seats."

I smile. "Their loss. It's lovely to meet you, Ella."

"You too." She lounges back against the plush, cream-colored seat. "Where do I know the name Caffrey from?"

"Nowhere good," I admit without hesitation, "although I try and do better than my predecessors."

Ella meets my eyes, searching, then gives a faint nod of approval at whatever she finds. "What would you recommend off the menu here?"

Choice in alcohol—or lack thereof—says a lot about a person, so I leave the spectrum wide. "They have trakal if you've never tried it. Their wine selection is good, especially if you like rosé. I like Hedonism—the whisky. But I'll cover anything you like off the menu, unless you prefer to pay for yourself."

A flicker of discomfort flits through her face, there and gone again. She's good at hiding it—I don't have to guess why. "Not going to buy me the most expensive bottle they can stuff a sheet of gold leaf into?"

"I wasn't planning on it. Money and pleasure only partially intersect, so I'd rather cater to your tastes over price. That way both of us can enjoy ourselves."

The flicker becomes a flame, burning behind Ella's eyes. She sighs, trying to hide the sound behind a sheepish smile.

"You seem nice, Sloane. And I legitimately mean that, because my father has tried to set me up with half the nouveau riche in Chicago, and all the ones before you were cis men with less personality than the mold growing underneath a fridge." Her lips purse. "But I only date women, and I have a feeling our lines don't quite intersect."

Oh. Clayton certainly didn't mention that. I've made a lot of people consider the flexibility of their preferences, but a firm boundary like Ella's isn't to be crossed.

"You're right. They don't." Which means taking a different tack entirely. "Your father doesn't know, does he?"

"No," Ella admits, "but I don't think it would make much difference. He'd just start looking for rich Wesleyan grads instead, and I don't need to be talked down to by a global studies major in a power suit during my off time. At least this way, the chances of running into my dates later at a club I like is low."

But she wants to make him happy, even if it means tolerating the occasional bad date. I can do a lot when 'single' and 'frustrated' are both on the table. "Understandable. But if I can ask, what is your type?"

She levels me with a hard look. "Depends on why you're asking."

"Because I know women in almost every profession and nearly every country, so I have to imagine between the two, there's someone out there with the exact lines that you're looking for. We're probably even friends."

Her brow tenses, betraying a split second of interest. "And what do you get out of playing matchmaker?"

I could lie, but chances are she would sense it. When cornered, I've found it's best to tell the truth, building a little bridge of honesty for whatever comes next. "Your father is presiding over a bidding war for one of the museum's exhibits. I want to be first in line to see Russell Key's photos. Do you know his work?"

Ella nods. "He came up tons in my research during my dissertation at Yale. You're a grad too, right?"

A common thread to pull—familiarity relaxes. "Class of 2012."

"2018 for me. My thesis involved research into how popular media enforces oversexualization for women of color. As you can imagine, his collections have had a lot of relevant papers written about them."

I'd argue most of Key's work qualifies, honestly. He liked testing the limits of American obscenity law. "What question were you trying to answer?"

"How much the digitization of media increased the effect. You could argue that Key only takes a single picture of one of his 'personal models', so it can't make that much difference in the sea of images we see every day. But in my analysis, he took millions. There's the original, the negative, and..." Her eyes meet mine, seeing if I'll find the answer.

"Countless copies," I say. "Every recreation is another piece with influence?"

"When you're famous as he was, absolutely. Even dead, he's making us run circles around each other to get a look." She chuckles softly. "But from the first shot to the last, there are stages of intention. Maybe she's naked in the original, but someone else throws a pixel censor over her breasts in the copy. A lot of people see what we spread to others as harmless, but I argue it's an active choice. A link isn't just a link when you're reinforcing cultural hegemony."

Maybe it's a good thing we don't play in the same league. I could dive into this debate for hours with pleasure, but that's not why I'm here. "And if you could take a picture of any one woman, what would she look like?"

Ella laughs, propping her hands up on the table and leaning in. "You really want to trade a hookup for a hookup, huh? What exactly does my father want from you?"

"As far as I could tell, your general interest. You tell him we hit it off, exchange a few texts, and play friendly until Friday."

She raises a brow. "The gala?"

I can't ask for a better alibi than being with the director's daughter for the evening. "Yes. We show up dressed to the nines together, share a couple flutes of champagne, then you change your mind Saturday morning. No harm, no foul."

"All of this because you want an early peek at Key's photos." Her gaze turns shrewd. "A lot of trouble for something so brief."

I smile, sheepish, as if she's caught me red-handed.

"Whoever your father picks also gets the sponsored plaque at the front of the exhibit. I like having my name inscribed on things, which I've interrogated in therapy for the last ten years to no avail. But if I can make the urge charitable, it's a little less mortifying."

People usually lie to make themselves look better. Embarrassing confessions are often taken at face value, acting as magnets for sympathy. Seducing Ella isn't on the table anymore, so coming off a touch pathetic is harmless.

After a long moment of silence, she sighs and gestures towards my phone. "You better have good taste in friends. And I want pictures—video, even. I refuse to get catfished by some gorgeous lesbian half a world away."

That won't be a problem. "Give me a profile, and I'll see what I can do."

Ella takes a moment to think about it, so we order our drinks. She settles on a cocktail laden with trakal, and my whisky arrives in a glass that fits perfectly in my hand. It's always a pleasure to experience the mastery of someone else's trade, especially when it isn't one I share.

"I'd like her to be around my age," Ella begins, squeezing a hint of lime into her drink. "I'm not going back to dating college students, and I don't need a sugar momma. Loving travel is a plus, but it has to be for a good reason—no misery tourism because she's sad about everything the locals are 'suffering'. I don't care about degrees. Real world experience means a lot more than the Ivy track. And for God's sake, I just want her to be interesting. Surprise me."

She's made my job so easy. I flip back a year in the gallery on my phone, picking out a pair of photos and the longest video on the list. "Then I think you and Joana Kachere would hit it off in an instant."

I slide my phone across the table so Ella can see the

screen. She taps it and the video starts, showing Joana giving a speech in front of several tons of captured ivory guarded by her fellow rangers. She pulls off a tailored khaki suit like she was born to wear a three-piece, switching between English and Chichewa without missing a beat.

"She runs a wildlife protection unit out of Lilongwe," I say when the clip ends. "Most of their work is in keeping elephants safe, but they have patrols around the rhino and lion reserves too. I've seen Joana scare off a dozen poachers with a single well-placed shot."

Ella's doing a terrible job not looking impressed. "Like the Akashinga? The women in Zimbabwe, I mean."

"Exactly. Joana was inspired by their mission, since Malawi has just as many issues with poaching. She founded the group, secured a chunk of government funding, and went to work. Illegal hunting in the region is down eighty percent."

"How did you even meet her?" Ella asks.

I found half a ton of ivory stolen from the region in the vault of a ninety-year-old ex-Nazi after a heart attack finally wiped him off the face of the earth, and thought Joana would enjoy burning his ill-gotten gains to ash. But that's too flashy of an explanation, so I say, "An investor I work with talked me into a wildlife tour that went across the whole continent. She's in charge of several tourism initiatives trying to convince rich hunters from the West to look and not shoot. We hit it off."

Ella wets her lower lip. "And Joana's out?"

I flick over to the pictures, showing her in a Jeep decorated with rainbow streamers. "She was the grand marshal for the first Pride parade in the city last year. But she doesn't really date local—there's a lot of politics involved.

She's given speeches in the States before, though, so you have a chance."

"Damn." Ella takes a very long sip of her drink. "Okay, Sloane. I'm interested."

Good. I much prefer setting up a woman for a nice date over breaking her heart in seventy-two hours. "I'll send you her WhatsApp. No promises, though. I'm a friend, not a love doctor."

"At this point, I'd be grateful for a conversation that doesn't bore me to death. Half the women in this city want to sell me on their yoga and crystals routine when we're supposed to be getting to know each other." She gives me a curious look. "So what's *your* type?"

Jillian, supposedly.

Before she burned me, I was on a dangerous line of thought, caught in a fantasy of soulmates being real. Nonsense, obviously, but I was starting to believe it. How many other women in the world could understand what I do and why I do it? I have to mask enough in my day-to-day; I refuse to live a lie for the sake of a relationship. Except there's not enough skill or pretty words to make up for what Jillian decided to do.

I still can't believe she called the fucking cops on me—the *feds*, no less.

Ella's staring at me, and I straighten up, realizing I answered her with a span of cold, dead silence. "Sorry. I... well, I like women that challenge me. But it gets me into a lot of trouble, so maybe I should stop biting off more than I can chew."

"You don't seem like the kind of person to settle down in some sparkling mansion with a trophy wife and some spoiled pet," Ella notes. "Would that really make you happy?"

Not even close. "Right now, a plaque in the Institute is going to make me happy. I'll work out the rest after that."

Her phone vibrates with a text, and she smiles. "It's Dad. Checking in on me, but also—you might want to see this."

Ella holds up her phone, and a picture of Clayton accompanies his message. He's holding a carefully wrapped print with one of the curators, and I instantly recognize both figures in the black-and-white photograph. Russell Key lays on a beach chair out in the sun, seemingly staring off into the light, while several phantoms of Adriana Azevedo—topless —surrounds him like a crown. The exposure work is incredible, but I can't call the concept anything but crude. She's just another object in his orbit, a would-be beauty queen crushed to dust and brightening Key's star.

But my bar-side analysis isn't important. This is proof the Institute has the photos in hand, and I recognize the Contemporary wing in Clayton's periphery. If they're putting the full exhibit together now, I'll have to strike soon. Using the gala as cover would be ideal, but I can't trust Jillian won't make a more aggressive move first.

"So close and yet still out of reach," I say. "Although it's a little grim, knowing Key might have killed his girlfriend."

"I don't like the guy very much, but he never struck me as a murderer." Ella locks her phone with a quick swipe. "From what I researched, his arrest yielded very little evidence and a *lot* of political motive."

Interesting. I'd never heard that before. "What kind of political motive?"

"Turns out most of the money everyone thought he dumped into a coke habit was going to some subversive groups in Brasília. It was the end of the eighties, a new wave of student organizations struggling against the dictatorship, that sort of thing. American dollars went far, especially since the CIA was backing the military at the time."

We just can't keep our noses out of other people's governments. "So you're saying someone set up a honeypot with him and Adriana?"

Ella shrugs. "Her body never turned up, and he fled before standing trial. I think he decided he'd rather be a celebrity over a revolutionary."

Explains why an entire box of very valuable photos were left behind in Brazil. Russell was booking it before they set him up to hang. "Not everyone's built to look down the barrel of a gun and laugh it off."

"You say that like you have personal experience," she notes. "Hiding a troubled past under that nice suit, Sloane?"

I grin. "Don't I wish."

Her laugh punctures the rest of the tension, so I relax too. After Ella finishes her drink, she pushes the cocktail glass aside. "Well, I appreciate you keeping me entertained even after I turned you down."

"You didn't turn me down completely," I counter.

"True. Which means you're meeting me in front of the Institute at five p.m. sharp." Ella looks me up and down. "And please don't embarrass us both by showing up in a basic-ass tuxedo."

I would never. "Deal."

Once she has Joana's information, I handle the bill and leave Ella to the rest of her evening. I've made plenty of progress, and I can't accomplish much else while the Institute's doors are sealed shut for the night.

Which is fine by me. After everything that happened today, I need some damn sleep.

CHAPTER II
JILLIAN

T enjoy heights.
　　Defying something as insistent as gravity satisfies
the ever-contrary spark burning in my heart, and it's
endlessly amusing how few people look *up*. I've been hooked
to a single cord on the side of a twenty-story skyscraper
above rush hour traffic before without incident, working my
way along window by window like I was the only human in
the world. The suspension of a good anchor point is akin to
flying, more liberating than any bondage advertised in edgy
clubs and droll magazine articles about finding the spice of
life.

　　The Institute is only four floors, but my safety measures
remain the same: maintenance-quality rope, a belay assist,
and a harness with quick release clips. Some recreational
climbers fear the latter, concerned they'll accidentally brush
against them at the wrong time, but I wear rescue gloves as a
matter of course, padded against friction burns if I have to
cut ties and suddenly drop a few stories the hard way, taking
the bag along with me. A thief's equipment gives away as

much about them as their presence; if you hide yourself but leave your gear behind, even the most brainless security guard can put two and two together.

My target is the roof of the Modern Art wing, but the Terzo Piano lounge on the same floor has far more tree coverage and looks out over a wide alley between buildings. Deliveries to the Institute move through there and enter at basement level, but without any available sidewalk, only a few guards seem to keep the street in their rotation. Once I'm locked in, I have about ten minutes to get to the top and secure my escape route out of sight.

Then the fun starts.

I brace myself with a glass gripper and start my ascent. They look like wildly exaggerated suction cups, but a small pump on the handle expels air between the rubber and whatever surface it's sticking to, sealing a bond that can survive half a ton of weight. A pair of these could get me to the top of Willis Tower if I had the inclination and enough time. Hell, Alain Robert did it in bare feet.

The gap between exterior cameras is only three feet wide, so I keep my shoes braced carefully against the glass, resisting any sway on the way up. Something about the pace is meditative—step, lean, clip, repeat. I find a stronger rhythm by the third floor, shaving off thirty seconds, and grip the lip of the roof with five minutes to spare. Crouched on the very edge, I pull up the ropes, take the carabiners off my harness—they're far too noisy at walking speed—and stash everything along with the gripper into the tightly zipped bag on my back.

Cameras aren't installed up here, but motion sensors sit embedded every six feet, little white bricks creating an active grid of surveillance. They're pyroelectric, searching for changes in heat—like say, the presence of a human body.

Light-based sensors are more reliable for catching an intruder, but they sense *everything*, from the motion of a wayward leaf to the wind blowing too hard. In Chicago, that makes the design useless, but pyroelectric devices have a weakness too: infrared energy barely registers through glass.

So all that's needed is a cube the size of my palm to hide the heat of my steps through lines of the grid; I use a Clichy paperweight swiped from Sotheby's. The space inside each square is harmless, resulting in a playful game of hopscotch to the double-layered roof of the Modern wing. It's a window higher than the lounge, easy enough to climb by hand, but as soon as I grasp the ledge, a burst of static from a radio freezes me in place.

"Check-in for blue team," the voice crackles, less than fifteen feet away from me. Weight shifts against steel in several places; at least four people, wearing heavy boots. "What's your status?"

Why the hell is there a squad on the *roof?* That wasn't in the rotation I listened to earlier, and it certainly isn't in the Institute's budget. You can't put just anyone on top of a building, not when there's a chance they'll fall off and open the managing company up to a massive workman's comp lawsuit. Such tactical training is left to military and police, not weekend warriors with guard cards.

"All clear." The one who answers has a clean alto timbre, commanding but frictionless, purposefully stripped of an accent. "Any noise downstairs?"

Another hiss of static. "Quiet as the grave."

No ranks, no typical radio codes. Who are these people?

I pull myself a scarce inch up over the edge of the roof, just enough to see. This late at night, the Institute is cast in shadow, but fractured light jumps from the towering buildings across the street. Four figures stand on alert—as expected—but their gear is black, patchless, and all-encompassing, offering no clue as to allegiance or identity. The pistols strapped to each hip say plenty about intent, though.

Damn it. This must be because of Sloane.

No one else knows my methods like they do, and no one else has the motive to warn the Institute about an unknown thief. They would never break in like this; hanging me out to dry won't sabotage whatever song and dance they're performing for the director—Woodward, I pluck from memory—and his fellows on the museum's board. While the crew of goons up here is busy guarding my way in, Sloane is probably seducing a keycard out of someone's purse.

My gut churns. We agreed on no police, but the group on the radio is too quiet and contained to be anything but professional. Maybe Woodward paid for a few nights of security from a private company; some of the American groups with industry contracts are little better than actual mercenaries, armed to the teeth and eager for a target. An operator might get sued for shooting at me, but a lawsuit is pointless if I'm dead.

Does Sloane hate me so much they'd risk me taking a bullet to make a point?

I can't be sure either way, which unsettles me enough to drop back down to the Terzo roof as quietly as possible. Tension wrenches up every inch of my spine as I creep over the motion sensors again, wary of the clunk of boots and safeties clicking off. The shift is about to change downstairs, so I spend five excruciating minutes waiting on the ledge, ready to throw myself over at the first sound of footsteps from behind.

Yet the guards below pass without incident, and my entry window has yet to close. I allotted forty minutes for climbing down through the third floor and mapping out the fastest path to Key's exhibit. With half that time left, I should be able to scout out the basement-side doors and if I'm lucky, pick up some useful chatter.

The descent is a simple anchor and slide down, so I loop through the alley and press against the corner where asphalt splits into concrete. An idling truck sits backed against the entrance as two men carry boxes out of the lower level, each one laden with scraps of wood and glass, broken tools and used brushes stacked on top. Paint-flecked pants and sweat-drenched shirts mark them both as construction crew, responsible for building new exhibits and dispensing of the old.

They also don't seem to have an escort. I can see into the hall behind the open doors, and while the far end has an imposing entryway, framed with concrete and a heavy steel grate, the front cage where a guard is supposed to be stands empty. To the left of it is a whiteboard covered from end to end with black marker, but I'm too far away to read the words squeezed in so close together in the half-light.

The guards I saw walking around were standard fare: black t-shirts and pressed trousers, profession written on their back and embossed right above one pocket on the chest. They carry radios, but no guns. I don't have the exact shirt, but I am entirely in black. With a quick change of shoes and my recorder clipped to my belt, the silhouette would be nigh-identical.

Sloane would walk right in and have both men wishing them good night on the way out. They're no better than me.

My backup tennis shoes are dark and soft-soled, nothing to write home about. I stick with common brands during break-ins; a unique footprint stands out too easily if law enforcement comes looking for evidence.

Once my bag is stashed in a shadow, I take a breath and round the corner. The men don't even notice me at first, too occupied with an unusually heavy frame. Part of blending in is setting the scene; if they catch me sneaking past, suspicion is inevitable.

"You guys need help with that?" I call out, pausing with a hand on my 'radio', as if to call for assistance.

"Nah, we're okay," says the taller of the two grunts, trying to adjust his grip on the frame. His partner doesn't even glance my way. "Thanks, though."

As they haul their burden into the truck, I walk past and into the basement hallway. Unfortunately, the guard cage is locked, but a glance through the screen reveals nothing more than a cramped space full of camera feeds and encroaching paperwork. Time sheets and incident reports, as far as I can tell.

The whiteboard is far more interesting. It's the crew schedule for the week, mired with abbreviations and other shorthand. I have to cross-reference a few rows before the code becomes clear: gold team handles the vault archives, red is assigned exterior security, and white is responsible for construction. White team names also have their own letters; I have to guess that the gentlemen outside are the two Ds for Disposal, and the CAs filling the rest of the row are busy in the Contemporary Art wing.

Interestingly, there is no 'blue' team like the group above mentioned, and no one seems to be assigned to the *inside* of the museum. If the Institute doesn't have the budget for a single guard milling around the lobby for a few hours a night, how can they pay the tactical unit loitering on the roof?

I have no answers, but I can't afford to linger. So I snap a quick picture of the whiteboard for reference, only to catch a pattern as the image loads. Andersen, one of the gold team members, is on vacation until Saturday.

If push comes to shove, I could pretend to be his replacement. Sloane must have warned them about my climbing expertise, but I don't usually do disguises. If I'm going to beat them at their own game, I might have to use similar tactics.

Takes a con to beat a con.

The clock is ticking, so I slip down the hall to take a picture of the door to the archives too, hanging just out of range from the camera above. I can study it later and find out what tools are necessary for a hard entry. Better safe than sorry.

One of the movers says goodnight to me on the way out, so I flash a smile in his direction, letting the expression fall once I'm out of eyesight. Irritation punches a deep crease deep between my brows, and I don't have the first idea of how to smooth it away.

But I can't do anything about that now. My first priority is getting back to the hotel without being caught.

CHAPTER 12

SLOANE

"You're cutting out a little bit, Clayton."

The director pauses, his pixelated face adjusting with the resolution before the image clears again. "Sorry. The reception on this floor is terrible."

He turns the phone camera towards a harried curator and the team of three she's overseeing for the Key exhibit. They've been arguing about print placement for most of the call, rearranging the order each time she mutters and shakes her head. Scans of the photos in question are barely visible on her tablet, and I want more than anything to reach through the screen and take it out of her hands.

"Not very exciting, I know," Clayton chimes in, the lens facing back his way, "but we're moving the pictures out of the vault tomorrow. Once they're in their frames, I'd love to give you a private tour."

I have no idea what Ella told her father about me, but he's been acting like I promised her a kingdom, and I'm content to play the part. "Is there something special about the frames? Most of his prints were pinned up in college dorm rooms back in the day. He never struck me as a formal kind of guy."

Clayton chuckles. "He wasn't. These pictures were stashed in a lockbox under his bed for years and exposed to who knows what kind of chemicals. Rondeaux had to write an entire protocol for handling them properly. I commissioned a custom case for each picture, and they cost a pretty penny."

Being too curious will tip my hand, but pretending ignorance serves in its stead. "Are you worried about light exposure? Acid in the paper?"

"All of the above." He glances up at the ceiling. "And honestly, vandalism. Controversial art tends to attract controversial behavior. So these are double-walled glass frames, magnetically locked in with a hydraulic seal in the base. Granite, of course, so it's heavy. No one's walking off with a photograph weighing two hundred pounds, and the top can't be pulled open by hand unless you're Superman."

Clever. And a long series of problems for me to solve. "And I imagine the seal is air tight. No exposure to the elements, and the glass keeps heat from getting through."

When Clayton nods, I bite my tongue. There must be a key for the frames—something physical—since including a battery element in every case to keep a digital lock running risks it running out of juice at the wrong moment. I'm passable at lockpicking, but having to do each one by hand would cost an outrageous amount of time. Sabotage from the outside demands a diamond-core drill bit, which is out of the question for the noise factor alone, and breaking the glass ruins my alibi.

At least the director's texts have been illuminating. Monitoring his phone has given me the full guest list for the gala on Friday and confirmation that no one else is to be given access to the Key photos outside the museum before then. Locking down access saves me at least one headache, although I'm concerned Jillian might try and steal the pictures when they're transferred from the vault to the frames.

Clayton mentioned having extra security on hand, although he didn't specify who, when, or where. They're not visible on the call, so I assume he either means more guards on the perimeter or a special escort on exhibition day. Hopefully, that will be more of a problem for Jillian than it is for me.

"I know the production aspect might look a bit boring on the outside," Clayton says, "but honestly, it's my favorite part. We're getting posters and banners delivered today, and once those are up, all this empty space is going to light up with color. I asked for a few special mirror displays too."

Interesting. "What kind of mirrors?"

"A bit of funhouse style. Like the pellicle in an SLR camera. Guests should see multiple reflections of themselves like in Key's work. Multiple exposure photos are easy now with electronic viewfinders and such, but he didn't have the tech back in his day."

I wonder if the motion sensors in the museum work off infrared. If so, Clayton may have just given me a way to turn invisible. "Brilliant. I can't wait to see everything come together."

"I've kept you for long enough, haven't I?" Clayton checks his watch. "God, it's nearly eleven. Get some rest, Sloane. I'll show you around tomorrow."

Until I actually see the photos, I can't do much else anyway. "Sounds great. See you tomorrow, Clayton."

The call ends, but I have no plans to sleep. I already spent most of the day sourcing materials to make high quality forgeries of Key's work, including a sealed box of paper from the eighties and MIT-grade photochromic ink. I don't expect the copies to hold up under intense scrutiny, but by the time the Institute gets an expert on site—if they ever figure out they've been robbed in the first place—I'll be long gone.

An ear-piercing shriek cuts through the hotel, high-pitched enough to make my teeth hurt. The red emergency light above the front door flickers to life, which is arguably better than the potential alternatives: white is a hostage situation, and blue is a bomb. Evacuating for a fire is annoying but tends to be less chaotic.

I have five minutes before Peninsula staff get up the stairs to hound me out of the room. More than long enough to store larger electronics and my chemicals in the disaster-proof safe; I reprogrammed the lock away from the default codes the day I got here, just in case. IDs go in the hidden pocket lining the right side of my suit, and everything else in my luggage is purposefully disposable.

A breathless attendant is at the end of the hall when I step out of the room, visibly relieved to see me. "This way, please! No need to panic. There was just a flare-up in one of the kitchens. You have our deepest apologies."

Poor man. He's used to people who take simple inconveniences as personal insults. "Is the fire department on the way?"

"Yes, but we have to ask our guests to remain outside until they give us the go-ahead." He forces a smile. "Stairs only, I'm afraid."

Reaching the bottom of the building is a bit of a hike, but by the time I'm down there, the other guests have been herded past the miniature botanical garden and out to the cool concrete of a maintenance lot. Several are in silk robes and complimentary Fendi sandals, clearly composing one-star reviews in their heads for the interruption, but beside a couple dressed to the nines, Jillian stands in a resolute column of black.

A loose t-shirt tossed over her stealth gear isn't enough to fool me. The imprint of a climbing harness lingers around both thighs, ruffled fabric and friction marks a dead giveaway. She must have been scouting out the Institute—did she see Clayton? Or did she get into the vault while everyone else was busy in the museum upstairs?

I need to find out, one way or another.

Jillian stiffens at my approach but doesn't move. Too many front-of-house staff from the Peninsula are watching to make sure we don't sneak back into the hotel and throw a fire code violation into the mix.

"I would have thought this was your fault," I say, gesturing to the building. "Pull an alarm, check out my room, and run off with the first important thing you find."

"If you were that simple to subdue, my life would be much easier." Real anger simmers in hazel eyes; the hour is too late for her to get away with sunglasses. "Who did you tell about the roof, hm? Siccing watchdogs on me is a new low."

I don't have the first idea what she's talking about, but I can't let her know that. Kudos to whoever Clayton hired if they managed to sniff someone like Jillian out so fast. "We agreed that anything goes, jewel. Are you having regrets? Because if you apologize to me, it would make your life *so* much easier."

"Apologize to *you*?" she snaps. "Is that what this is about? Pushing me into a corner until I humiliate myself?"

Now it is. Last time I tried to imagine a better future between us, she ripped it out from under me and spit in my face. "I used to play nice. We were good together. It felt incredible."

Her lips purse. "You don't own me just because you touched me once, Caffrey."

"Twice." No point in dignifying the rest with an answer. "We had sex twice."

Jillian stares at me. "No, we didn't. Once in Paris was more than enough, thank you."

For a second, I feel like I'm losing my mind. If not for the fact that those memories are branded in my body to the bone, her insistence might shake me. "You're joking. Are we only counting penetration? Did you turn Catholic when I wasn't looking? Because being holier-than-thou really doesn't suit you."

She rolls her eyes. "If you're looking for a blow-by-blow to get off to when you curl up in that big penthouse bed alone tonight, you won't get it from me."

I don't care about the sex. I care that it was *her*. "All night, Jill. We slept a little while, until sunrise. Then, I had you again."

"It's called a one-night stand, no matter how long it lasts," Jillian hisses under her breath. "Fluff your ego however you like, but it was the same encounter. Once. One too many times. And I'm not sure why we're even arguing when it was the biggest mistake of my life."

The venom in her voice sinks deep. For a second, I'm calm, and the next my blood is burning. No antidote exists save biting back.

"Right. Because I remember the way you begged. We couldn't even get our clothes off at the start because you dragged my hand up your skirt. The little sob of relief when I finally found out how wet you were. Hours and hours of taking you over the edge until you were so sensitive you could barely stand for me to touch you. And you still wanted more. So how about we count how many times I made you come?"

If I'm ablaze, Jillian is absolute zero, leveling me with a cold and culling look. She's so still, I'm not sure she's even breathing until her hands squeeze into white-knuckled fists. I want to dare her to wrap her hands around my throat, just to laugh when she takes pleasure in touching me again.

"Oh, Caffrey. You think about that night so much more than I do." Her voice is even, empty of feeling. "Were you convinced you were the best I ever had? That I've been wasting away without you? Because I assumed a lady-killer like yourself would know when a woman fakes an orgasm."

"You—" No. She's fucking with me. "You didn't fake a damn thing."

"After months of build-up, I expected more, but you were so enthusiastic." Jillian holds my gaze without hesitation, and I hunt for any sign of a lie. "I didn't want to ruin the mood. But you did that yourself the morning after, so I suppose there's no reason to hold back now."

I taste acid. She doesn't blink or redirect, shoulders slack like we're having a conversation about our favorite colors. Without the curtain of propriety between us, Jillian isn't even angry. She's *pitying* me.

Why am I doing this? Chasing after her like some masochistic fool, when the night that meant everything to me was apparently a farce she doesn't care to remember. I wanted to make Jillian happy by her rules—always by her fucking rules—and couldn't even manage that. No wonder she turned on me. I never had a chance. Her heart can't belong to anyone else when she keeps sole custody.

"Please return to your rooms!" one of the attendants calls

out. "Again, we're so sorry for the interruption. Room service will be complimentary until ten a.m."

Only a life of iron-clad self-control stops me from bolting towards the hotel.

"You're right," I say, forcing past the tightness in my chest, the tourniquet trying to hold everything together after Jillian gut me. "No reason at all."

Before she can say another word, I move to leave and catch a woman in the Peninsula's doorway staring at us. She's average height, standing level in a pair of heavy black boots tucked up under matching slacks. A loose shirt like Jillian's drapes down her body, mirrored by waves of sepia curls, bunched with the signs of a hastily stripped ponytail. I don't recognize her, but from the curiosity in vivid blue eyes, I'm not sure the feeling's mutual.

One of the hotel staff taps her shoulder, and she turns around with a smile, disappearing as the crowd of guests floods back into the lobby.

Great. The last thing I need in the middle of this heist is more attention.

CHAPTER 13

JILLIAN

T went too far.

When Sloane falls from view, I relax my hands, but the sting of salt and blood remains. I punctured a full set of crescents into one palm, using the pain to hide every sign of deception. It's a trick I haven't used in years, not since a border agent in Italy detained me on a lark. Sloane's sabotage wasn't the cause on that particular occasion; said agent simply saw a young, attractive woman traveling alone and wanted to put me in a box to see what would happen. If not for the Tintoretto painting concealed in my luggage, I would have accepted the assault charge just to spit in his face.

Except I don't lie to Sloane. I never have. They looked like they were about to throw up before walking away, except the sickness was self-directed. Something in me snapped; I was tired of exchanging jabs and having them deflected. I wanted to pierce their armor, that adamantine pride, just once. Telling the truth would have only bolstered Sloane, made them untouchable.

Our one night was never *one night*. What point is there in trying to count how many times release happened between us when I lost track after the first hour? They were ravenous in their worship, as if I was the only woman on earth, more valuable than anything we could ever steal. Of course I begged, because when Sloane dove beneath the surface and saw everything I was, they were happy to drown.

And I touched them too. They surrendered to me, fearless of the fall, of what I might see, say, think. If I could have buried myself inside Sloane's chest in those hours, I would have, embedded like gold in a catacomb saint. We had more than pleasure; it was a reckoning, a line of connection I never thought I could have with anyone else.

We *were* good together. We were perfect. So why didn't they stay?

I woke up just after ten a.m. in Paris to a cold and empty bed, every sign of their presence erased. If not for Sloane's fading scent on the pillow beside me, it would have been easy to believe they were never there at all.

But then I found the note. Folded in half, written on paper from the hotel, pointed towards the bed like an arrow. Mere hours after Sloane ruined me for anyone else, they ruined me again with ten little words.

Thanks for the fun, jewel. Catch you again some time.

I was another checkbox in a long list of conquests: destroy their family, steal a painting from every Old Master, bed Jillian Rhodes. If they simply left, I probably would have fallen over myself to justify it—someone called them away for a last-minute job, I'd been too clingy, they had a complex about sharing a bed—but the note evaporated every last drop of doubt.

They didn't call or text that day, or the next, despite having the only phone number I kept with any permanence. By the time Sloane resurfaced, they were raiding a dead man's treasure trove, and I hadn't heard a word. I knew that even if they didn't care about me, they cared about their reputation, and I put in a call to a local thief in Germany, mentioning I knew an 'art dealer' who would be walking around with a suitcase full of sketches.

A petty, half-baked revenge. I expected them to turn up at my doorstep within a week demanding an explanation so that I could do the same. Instead, I ended up stuck in the backwoods of an airport by Sisteron, because every credit card associated with my Parisian alias had been canceled simultaneously. I grit my teeth and pulled cash from a deeply buried emergency fund to hire a private pilot before the Gendarmerie showed up to investigate me for multiple counts of fraud.

I could have let it stop there, an eye for an eye, but Sloane had told me everything. I know their hideaways, their favorite haunts, how many languages they speak and how well. If pressed, I could write out an entire Caffrey family tree back to their origins in Dublin, cousins included. Everything they love is permanently etched into my mind, and if I'm not on that list, then making them pay for the burden of such knowledge comes second best.

But I never imagined retaliation would put a look on their face like the one I just saw, heartsick, as if the organ was fruit dying on the vine. For Sloane, this is just a game, isn't it? Another victory to claim, their certificate of ownership inked in my misery.

Fingertips brush my elbow. "Miss?"

I hate when strangers touch me, but it's one of the hotel attendants, and the dead quiet around us snaps into sharp relief. I'm the only guest standing in the lot, and the last fire truck is trundling back down the main thoroughfare, sirens off.

"Sorry." I try to smile, but it doesn't stick. The museum climb and Sloane were two high spikes of adrenaline, and now that they're both gone, exhaustion hollows me from the inside out. "Too much on my mind."

She offers to send a cup of relaxing tea up to my room, but I decline and keep walking. The lobby is still flush with staff, and so many eyes on me at once is unsettling. With the elevators working again, it's a quick ride up to my room—a single floor below Sloane's treasured penthouse.

When the doors slide open, the temptation to let them close again and press the top button possesses me. They're probably sulking with a glass of bourbon; despite numerous attempts, I was never able to sell them on scotch.

Would they let me in? What would they do if I let myself in?

I imagine Sloane pinning me back against the door, strong hands knowing exactly where to grip. They could punish me or kiss me; I deserve the first, but I wouldn't refuse the second. Wounded or not, I know what their mouth is capable of. Maybe if I let Sloane have me again, the pain of the first time would lose its edge, the same way a new cut blunts the scratch of old scars, no matter how deep.

The elevator dings in frustration, eager to move on.

Fuck.

I step out of the car before I can convince myself otherwise and head straight to my room. When I open the door, the coin I left angled against the bottom is in the middle of the carpet, shoved out of place by someone coming in. Hotel staff are legally obliged to check rooms for wayward guests during emergencies, but I do a careful inventory of my belongings just in case. Nothing incriminating was out in the open, of course; I know better than to scout a heist while leaving evidence in an unattended room tied to my name.

Everything is intact and seemingly untouched, so I throw my backpack on the bed and strip down, eager to wash the sweat off my skin. Rooms in the Peninsula come with an egregiously large tub, but a long soak is asking to get maudlin at this point. The shower has plenty of luxury in its own way, a cradle of wood and stone that sends water flowing down like the gentle kiss of rain, with more pressure and temperature adjustments than the International Space Station.

I close my eyes and mentally walk a path through the Institute, connecting stairwells and floors to their twins. The elevator in the back of the Contemporary Art wing might become my main entryway since the roof is off limits. If I forge a serviceable copy of that key tomorrow, I can access the photos from anywhere they happen to be.

The vault door itself is a different story. I'll need to blow up the picture I took in detail, but there was at least one camera and a matching motion sensor. Materially speaking, it's heavy enough to subvert most basic kinds of brute force —hammer, car, bomb—but the main lock was digital. I'd bet a bottle of Macallan 30 the panel uses Bluetooth, which means a sniffer can suss out the passcode in a matter of seconds. If not, I can always spoof the alarm. How security companies convinced anyone storing vital information in the cloud was a good idea, I'll never know.

And that's if I even need to go down there. Disguising myself as Andersen's temporary replacement should provide access to the entire museum; people rarely question the presence of guards for fear that it will draw suspicion to themselves, and agencies turn out new employees every week to keep up contract quotas.

Timing is the only variable left. The schedule didn't list when Key's collection was being moved out of the vault, and showing up in the middle of a shift would be a red flag. I can arrive before closing hours in civilian wear and leave the recorder in my purse again, but with a live feed this time. When the doors lock for the day, I'll change and enter with the next shift. With less than forty-eight hours until the exhibit opens, chances are the pictures will be on display already, and I can crack any case on the market.

Which makes me curious what exactly the Institute has up their sleeve. Nothing I've seen so far is particularly impressive. Hell, it's almost amateurish. Russell Key Jr. could have hired a thief with half my expertise and still have had a good chance of getting what he wanted.

Either way, stealing the photos first is what matters. If I focus on the pictures instead of Sloane, my life will be a hundred times easier.

I may not enjoy always being alone, but it's so much less complicated. My instincts never lead me astray.

Never, except when it comes to Sloane.

CHAPTER 14

SLOANE

The Contemporary Art wing has been completely transformed.

Blank white walls are now awash with color, overlapping neon silhouettes of Key's profile guiding the eye towards the exhibit. A massive media collage showcases decades of his most famous magazine covers and prints, along with paperwork and video clips from associated obscenity lawsuits. The mirror toy Clayton mentioned sits on wheels in an adjacent corner, a six-foot-tall hexagon booth reflecting at every angle, allowing passersby to duplicate themselves on a whim.

Across from the main gallery is a display on Key's politics and his murder arrest, encouraging the viewer to draw their own conclusions as to why he fled from Brazil. Underneath the descriptive placard is a note in small, italicized text: *With consultation and research by Ella Woodward.*

She texted me this morning to say Joana is "like someone out of her wildest dreams," so if I ever need a fallback for the thief business, matchmaking might be my go-to. Fixing other people's relationships is far easier than managing my own.

Clayton awaits me outside the glass doors to the gallery. A velvet rope is meager protection to separate this wing from the rest of the busy museum, but since the Institute is about to close, I suppose they're less concerned about the curious wandering in. Such overconfidence is exactly why art theft remains lucrative; relying on public goodwill is no replacement for a proper security system.

The doors aren't even *locked*.

"Sloane! Good to see you." He holds a set of keys in hand; one has a rounded base, heavy with a magnet. "Ready for the big reveal?"

"You've had me on edge the whole week," I joke, following him past the glass doors.

Compared to the riot of chaotic imagery outside, the gallery itself is almost sedate. Two motion sensors face each other on opposite walls, their infrared eyes a dead giveaway by color alone. A single camera hangs above the entryway, angled down towards visitors but leaving a swathe of the room unattended. While the center of the room is a hotspot of surveillance, every corner offers invisibility, with narrow paths along each side.

Clayton's vaunted frames, on the other hand, look like a much larger problem. Four are arranged horizontally in the middle of the room, granite bases holding them up in the form of heavy gray columns; the other two take up a wall each. He undersold the size—they're three hundred pounds apiece, easy. The pictures themselves are matted under glass, held in place, and the glass itself is thick enough to survive a sledgehammer. A steel lock guards the front of each frame where its hollow top meets granite, preventing brute force from shattering the hydraulic seal.

Clayton clears his throat. "What do you think?"

Right, I'm supposed to be in awe. "This is incredible."

In a technical sense, Key was a master of his art. The photo closest to me is in black and white, with Adriana Azevedo sitting on the beach and facing the camera. Shoulder-length hair, flat iron perfect, cuts a dark line through the center of the image, but the focus is on her eyes, a piercing stare captured in sharp, perfect detail. Adriana has such a familiar face, the kind you see once on a poster and never, ever forget. Her dress is divided by a sharp V, baring skin from throat to belly button, but its palm tree pattern is reflected in the same trees behind her, holding the true shock of the image. Multiple exposures of Key himself silhouette the horizon, nigh-invisible on first glance. His body is cut through with heavy fronds and spiky trunks, appearing like an illusion above the sand.

The title on the card below is surprisingly sentimental: *Love Takes Root.*

"Do you mind if I snap my own pictures?" I ask, holding up my phone.

"You're welcome to. No flash, of course." His brows press together in a serious line. "But if these leak to the media or anyone else before Friday, I'll have you on the hook for a lot more than five million dollars."

Lucky for him, I don't want anyone ever finding out what I have on my phone. "Understandable. I just want to enjoy Key's art without the crowd."

I haven't even cut him a check for the plaque yet, but such is the purview of the obscenely wealthy—making demands while holding the promise of money just out of reach. At this point, I don't care if I have to pay the Institute for the sake of maintaining my cover; the second Jillian became involved, profit stopped being a priority.

Clayton smiles. "Then, please. Feel free."

The other photos are in color. One of them, entitled *Envy*, has Key and Azevedo naked and facing each other in full profile, echoes of their bodies expanding out past the edges of the photograph. Despite the countless physical differences between them, they both have blue eyes: his leaning towards shallow seawater, hers deep and stunning as azurite. His blonde scruff and sunburned skin are no surprise, but neither is her waxed and tanned perfection—beyond a set of sculpted eyebrows and dark brown hair spilling in a glossy curtain over one shoulder, Adriana is obsessively smooth.

I wonder if Russell ever figured out what exactly he was envious of.

While taking shots, I murmur commentary off the top of my head to Clayton so he focuses more on my opinion of the crude artistry behind Key's magnum opus—has a cishet man ever made a piece called *Orgy* without giving away endless psychosexual hang-ups?—than my meticulous documentation of the gallery. One photograph against the wall is poorly lit, but it gives me an idea.

"The glare off the glass here is terrible," I say, pitching sympathy into my voice. "Anyone taking pictures is going to go blind."

Clayton walks over to where I'm standing and frowns. "I'll have to have Marian tweak the lights. Although with the rounded edge of the glass, that might not make much of a difference."

"It's also an inch thick," I note. "But maybe if I try..."

With each failed photo, I sigh in unvoiced frustration, fussing with the settings on my phone like it will suddenly unlock a code. Clayton's awkwardness grows, bit by bit, until he puts a light hand on my arm.

"Let me open the case. You can take a picture, and I'll seal everything back up."

The hardest part of my job is not smiling when people walk right into the trap I've put down. "Oh! Sure, that would be great."

He inserts the magnetic key at the bottom of the case and twists it hard. "I have to be careful not to accidentally put any of my other keys in here. The repulsing magnet inside will just keep it permanently stuck. A clever anti-theft measure, but as someone who carries around a ring of near-identical keys..."

Very clever. Making a mold of the key isn't enough to defeat the lock, and evidence of the attempt is left behind.

A soft hiss emanates from the case as the hydraulic hinge opens, pushing the glass up and out of the way. With the case open, seeing the machinery inside is easy, but no thief poking around from the outside would have any idea what they were up against; it collapses down into the granite base when the seal is shut.

I need Clayton's key.

So I drop down onto one knee, intent on taking my photo up close, and snap several shots before standing up in a rush. The point of my elbow seeks the center of his forearm, and his grip goes slack, sending the ring tumbling to the floor with a clatter of steel and brass.

"I'm so sorry," I mutter, grabbing the keys and feeling around for my prize.

The magnetic base is the size and weight of a watch battery, embedded in the bow of the key. Small but industrial strength—Clayton's steel set resists gravity to stay close, but the brass ones don't react in the least. I've seen something exactly like it in EVVA MCS locks, designed to be unpickable.

Since the magnetic field is unique, it's impossible to make a copy unless you study the particular key in question.

Clayton takes his keyring back with grace, playing off my awkwardness. "Is there anything else in the Institute you'd like to look at? I'd be happy to take you to any of the other galleries."

"I've kept you here long enough." I smile, gesturing at the time on my phone. "Why don't we call it a night?"

I watch him seal the case again, making a quick recording behind his back. This jaunt should have provided the information I need, but an abundance of caution has always served me well. The smallest speed bump during a heist can derail the entire operation, even if the damage isn't immediately obvious. Just because you grab what you came for doesn't mean you haven't left behind enough evidence to get caught.

"I assume I'll see you at the gala," Clayton says as we walk out to the lobby together.

"Of course. Ella made it clear I wasn't supposed to wear a tux."

He chuckles. "I'm just glad you two hit it off. She's had a hard time dating in the past, and well, honestly... she has very high standards."

Her standards start and end with women. Having skin in the game is difficult when you're not qualified to play. "She's gorgeous, brilliant, and a Yale grad. I think I'd be worried if her standards weren't high."

Clayton gives me a curious look then nods. "True. And it's not like I want her to undersell herself. I just—I don't want her to end up alone."

With any luck, he'll have a daughter-in-law inside of a year; Joana is very serious about commitment. "You love her, Clayton. Trust me, I'm not judging."

He sees me off at the velvet rope, so I leave through the front door. On my way out, I loop the building, marking a line of motion sensors on the layered glass roof—and the edge of black boots.

I freeze. Between the line of trees and deep shadows projected from the building, a tactical rope connects to the roof, several color-coded carabiners clipped to the anchor on top. The boots move, falling out of sight, and my jaw tightens. Imagining Jillian waltzing around above my head this entire time pulls at the core of anger in my chest, drawn hot and thin and twisted as molten glass.

She made me feel so goddamn *vulnerable* last night. I woke up and got ahold of every bit of protection I could get on short notice, even topping off my lawyer's retainer. Kimberly Lei Shen is well into her seventies now, but she took me seriously as a teenager when I brought Caffrey Chemical's breaches to her attention, which is how I set my family for a precipitous fall from grace. Trusting her with my life and freedom is easy—I wish it was that simple with anyone else.

I close the distance to the rope with silent steps. My driving gloves aren't ideal for climbing, but I'm not inclined to leave DNA on anything belonging to Jillian. One hard pull gets me off the ground before I hook the rope around one leg and brake with the other, keeping my foot under the slack. I'm no cat burglar, but the technique is simple, if somewhat dangerous without a harness.

Adrenaline takes me past the first floor of the Institute, then up to the second. I have no idea what I'm going to even say to her, but the look on her face when I interrupt her late-night infiltration will be enough of a victory. We agreed anything goes, so there's nothing stopping me from direct sabotage. If she wants to throw a real fit, then we'll both get arrested. She can sink to the bottom with me.

I have to pause for a breath just below the roof. The tight weight beneath my suit is much heavier when I'm holding myself up by core and arm strength alone, layered over a dress shirt that's now soaked with sweat.

With a grunt, I push my feet against the wall of the building and hoist myself over the wall of the roof, making the carabiners violently jangle.

A figure in black whips around: masked and two inches taller than Jillian.

Every other detail is sublimated by the gun pointing straight at my chest. An M&P Shield, safety off.

It fires, cutting the world into bright, explosive pieces.

CHAPTER 15

JILLIAN

I press my fingertips against the back of a silicone mold, and a perfect copy of the elevator key pops out, made of new, clean plastic.

This is the last piece of the plan, barring whatever I have to do to free the photos from their frames, but I have a range of options laid out on the bed: glass cutter, diamond-tipped drill, and a ceramic blade sharp enough to pierce anything under a 6 on the Mohs Scale. I don't care if the Institute knows they've been robbed, so long as I'm gone before the realization occurs. Once Russell Key Jr. has the photos in hand, they're going to be ash anyway.

A hard thud through the ceiling startles me so much, I almost drop the mold. I glare upward, wondering what the hell Sloane is doing above me, but the next sound is suspiciously solid, body-heavy. The silence that follows puts my teeth on edge, but the swell of concern in my chest is doubly frustrating.

Their business shouldn't be any of mine. After the last three years, Sloane has made that abundantly clear, but between an ill-advised urge to care and the same damnable curiosity that drew me to them in the first place, I get up and leave my room. If they're in trouble, I'll be justified, and if Sloane decided to stomp on the floor like a child in order to irk me, I'm giving them a piece of my mind.

I've been copying hotel keys since I was a teenager, but the Peninsula uses an app for access to exclusive floors. While it imposes another barrier on anyone who can't afford a cell phone, it took me less than twenty minutes to dig into the program and find out the only thing stopping anyone from reaching the penthouse was flipping a single variable from NO to YES. So I angle my false entry code to the black screen above the floor buttons, and it welcomes me with a cheery beep before the elevator rises.

The penthouse hallway is painted in soothing oceanic blue, but my shoulders go rigid when I see the door at the end of it is ajar. No matter my personal feelings about Sloane, they're an incredible thief and utterly meticulous about their own security.

Maybe I should have brought the knife.

Keeping my steps feather-light, I step past the open door, only to recoil at the scent of dry, scorched skin. The culprit is a pair of driving gloves on the marble entryway, leather palms shredded open by rope burn. Smooth white stone gives way to ivory carpet, and collapsed in the center of spotless luxury is Sloane, curled up on one side and breathing hard.

The first thud must have been from the sealed bottle of whisky on the floor, but they've given up on reaching for it, uttering a pained curse under their breath. Sulfur suffuses the air, emanating from a dark, jagged tear in the breast of Sloane's jacket.

Who *shot* them?

I'm beside Sloane on my knees before I can think otherwise, trying to guide them onto their back. I don't see or smell blood, but out of pure panic, I rip their jacket open, tugging at the dress shirt underneath until tortoise-shell buttons pop.

"Jillian—" they gasp.

"Who did this?" I snap. It comes out vicious as my hands find the burned black threads of a bulletproof vest with the bullet in question lodged an inch above Sloane's heart. Small caliber, but that's little comfort. "Jesus."

"I thought it was you," Sloane grits out before managing to sit up, the movement breaking my touch. "Clocked that it wasn't a bit too late."

Relief over the fact that they're alive is washed away by a wave of outrage. "You thought I would *shoot* you?"

"You didn't see the look on your face last night." They shrug out of the remains of their jacket, wincing when their left shoulder is forced to shift. "I realized 'anything goes' didn't leave any caveats for bodily harm. First time I've actually tested this vest, so I'm glad it works."

The hint of humor in Sloane's voice leaves me cold. My entire body is frigid with disbelief. "I would never, ever hurt you like this."

Their mouth twitches into a thin line. "Is pulling the trigger yourself where you draw the line? Because you were happy to sic Interpol on me a year ago."

What? Maybe the pain is making them delirious.

"I don't call the cops. You know that."

Green eyes narrow with renewed viciousness as Sloane pushes away from me, leaning back against the wall instead. They start to remove their vest with prejudice, ripping the Velcro straps open one by one despite an obvious twitch of agony.

"Don't lie to me." With red, sweat-damp hair hanging around their face, Sloane looks every inch the wounded lion. "Elias Denning, the only man I've ever heard you call a 'friend', put a blue notice on my name before having the Spanish police arrest me. Four charges of theft across international lines is almost half a century in prison."

No. What?

I've known Elias for a decade. He's a capable fence and has never led me astray, not once. I would know if he was Interpol. I couldn't possibly miss—

"Kimberly got the notice revoked and the charges dropped for lack of evidence," Sloane continues, "but I was detained for fourteen hours. Just my luck to be a rich American they could throw in a solitary cell, because I can only imagine how they would find out whether to house me with women or men."

Nausea twists my stomach. God, no wonder they hate me. I'm the only connection between Sloane and Elias, and I've bad-mouthed them to him more than once. Something I said must have clued Elias in to one of Sloane's thefts-in-progress.

But I didn't suspect a goddamn thing.

"You—" Sloane swallows hard, and the dread tearing me apart from within suddenly reflects in their eyes. "Fuck. *You* didn't know? Jill, you're the one who taught me how to spot the feds. I learned everything from you."

"I had no idea." My voice comes out distant, despairing. I've been so obsessed with Sloane using me, the notion of someone else being capable of such a thing never crossed my mind. A horrible question bursts out of me: "Is he in Chicago? Is he the one who shot you?"

"You would know better than I would," Sloane says, the anger in their voice tempered by sudden sympathy. My heart curls in on itself like crumpled foil. "But no, I don't think so. He's a hair over five ten, and whoever pulled the trigger didn't clear five six."

"He texted me," I realize belatedly. Shock is slowing me down; I need to snap out of it, get ahead of this. "A few days ago, asking what I was up to. I was vague, of course, but that doesn't matter. Interpol could relay a warrant to ping my phone in minutes."

Sloane shifts and flinches. "Help me get the vest off. I need to see what the damage is."

It's not a request, but I can't blame them for a lack of manners, considering the circumstances. I pull the vest up over Sloane's head, then hiss under my breath at the mosaic of black and blue bruises underneath, spreading from their collarbone and over the rise of their chest. By some mercy, the skin isn't actually broken anywhere, and as far as I can tell, the bones beneath aren't either. Yet I can't shake the horrifying truth that it was a lethal shot, prevented only by their reflexive precaution.

The urge to touch Sloane, to comfort them, is dizzying. Three years since I've had my hands on their body, since I fell asleep against Sloane's chest, listening to their heartbeat. I bite my tongue.

"Tell me more about the shooter," I say, determined to distract myself. "Where did this happen?"

"On the roof of the Institute." Sloane tugs the bottle of whisky into their lap. "I was inside with the museum director, and when I came out, I saw boots and a climbing rope down the back wall."

No wonder they assumed it was me. "And they shot you from the roof?"

A wry smile bares Sloane's teeth. "No. I climbed up there to give you a piece of my mind and ruin your night."

"Without a harness?" I hiss. Those ruined gloves are probably the only reason Sloane survived a hard slip down the rope. "Do you not have a single survival instinct left in your body, Caffrey? Free climbing buildings is for *experts*, and I still don't do it unless I absolutely have to."

"Okay, expert," they growl back, "then tell me why the hell anyone else but you would be up there."

I was sure Sloane was responsible for the squad on the roof. But if not, we have a much bigger problem. Elias might only be the beginning. "Because someone at the Institute pulled strings to have a personal paramilitary unit watching for break-ins at the top of the building."

Sloane blinks twice. "Excuse me?"

"The first time I cased the museum, I saw them lurking over the Modern Art wing. Which is strange because it's closed for construction. They wouldn't have any reason to be there, except to stop a thief from going through that floor down to the Contemporary galleries underneath."

They let out a dry chuckle, then wince. "Where Russell Key's photos are being displayed."

I nod, and Sloane wrenches the cap off their whisky. "I'm trying to complete a thought, but this hurts too damn much for me to think. One moment."

Their tolerance is high, but it's still impressive to watch Sloane down several shots worth of 105 proof liquor in a continuous swallow. I'm twice as surprised when they offer me the bottle, but I shake my head. One of us has to stay sober for this.

"So." Sloane clears their throat. "What's the chance that fire alarm was a fakeout?"

Jesus Christ. "High. Extremely high."

"I agree. But I came back to my room and searched it after. Nothing I own had been moved, and everything important was locked up. I assume the same is true for you."

"Of course. I use an ORION for counter-surveillance too, and there weren't any bugs left behind on my end."

"Because Denning—and whoever he's working with—knows we're both paranoid." When I open my mouth to protest, Sloane insists, "Rightfully so. But they would plan for it."

"Except they wouldn't need a twenty-four hour stream of what we're doing in the hotel," I murmur. "They just need to know when we're here and when we're gone."

I push to my feet without thinking, then duck over to Sloane's doorway and stare through the peephole. Right above the elevator is a dime-sized black square attached to the emergency exit sign like a battery output, but I know better.

"One camera is on your side of the elevator," I say. "I'd bet my hallway has one too. But the Peninsula doesn't use devices that size. Which means they saw me come up here and inside your room."

"Yet they haven't swept in to arrest us both." As Sloane speaks, I triple check the locks, then put a good length of distance between myself and the door. "Which is fair. I don't think they have any evidence we've committed any crimes yet."

"Technically, you were trespassing on the roof," I counter.

"I was visiting the Institute at the director's invitation." Sloane raises a brow. "I didn't break or enter. And whoever was on the roof *shot* me."

"But it wasn't Denning?"

"No." Their eyes widen slightly. "No, it wasn't, but..."

Sloane swaps the whisky for their phone and starts to flip

through its photo gallery with rapid swipes of one thumb. They look up at me during the search, then back to the pictures, before staring at me again.

"I need to put my hands on you," they say.

My heart crashes into the front of my chest. "What? Why?"

After a second's pause, Sloane confesses: "To take your measurements."

I swear, if this is a joke— *"Why?"*

Sloane braces themself against the wall and manages to stand. "Because I'm going to compare you to another woman. Sorry, jewel, you're the only model in the room right now."

I really should have brought the knife. "If you are messing around in any way..."

"I'm not." Their voice drops low—hard, serious. "I think I know who shot me, but I have to be absolutely sure."

I've lied to them, but Sloane has never lied to me. If this entire mess is because of Elias, then I owe them, much as it stings to admit. Logically, the equation is sound, but the flush of adrenaline that pours through my body isn't rational. I'm scared for them to touch me again; I don't know what will happen.

But Sloane took a bullet. I can handle a little fear.

"Don't get cute," I mutter and step into their personal space.

Sloane doesn't answer, but their gaze turns sharp and analytical. Their fingertips start at my brow, brushing feather-light down my nose, then over the shape of my cheek. The contact is unspeakably gentle, so slow it could be mistaken for a caress if not for the fact that Sloane keeps checking their phone between every pass along my skin.

When their hand falls down my throat and over the line

of my shoulder, I barely hold in a shiver. Sloane draws a finger past my bust and ribs without so much as a pause or smile, then stops at the juncture of my hip.

"Well, if nothing else," Sloane says, "I think I've just solved a murder."

CHAPTER 16

SLOANE

Giving Jillian a proper explanation takes longer than I want, but that's the downside of stumbling into an actual conspiracy—you sound completely out of your mind unless every single point of context is explained. Even as the words leave my mouth, I'm convinced she's going to laugh and leave me hung out to dry, but by the end, I can see gears spinning in her head, the clockwork of intellect that makes her so damn brilliant.

"This whole thing is a con," I finish. "So what are we going to do about it?"

She pinches the bridge of her nose and sighs. "The first thing I'm doing is patching you up. No one can know you were shot. We need the truth as a card up our sleeve."

My throat tightens. Touching her was difficult enough a minute ago; I'm not sure I can handle Jillian's hands on me. "I'll do it."

"You can barely move your shoulder on that side." Hazel eyes narrow. "Let me help. I don't feel any better about this than you do, Sloane."

Ouch. Even the bullet didn't have three years' worth of sting.

"Glad you still remember my name," I mutter.

She swallows hard, a flash of anxiety there and gone again. It must have been an accident, emotion getting the better of her for once.

"Don't start," Jillian whispers. "Just... come on."

Tension simmers in the pit of my stomach as I follow Jillian into the bathroom. I sit on the edge of the tub when she takes the first aid kit out from under the sink. Trying to keep my shoulder locked and still while having her move around me is far more distracting than bruises, no matter how severe.

She breaks down the entire kit with an EMT's expertise, dividing out what she needs while reorganizing the rest. After popping the capsule inside an ice pack, Jillian offers it to me with a brusque, "Hold this."

I do until she grabs a towel from the rack, wrapping the ice tight before placing it against my chest. The pressure comes across as a strange haze of pain filtered through the whisky and slowly numbed out by cold. I shiver, but Jillian redirects my hand to keep the pack in place, her fingers overlapping mine.

"Ten minutes here," she mutters, then grabs the emergency scissors to start dividing a roll of elastic bandages into long strips. "I'm... sorry about Elias."

The apology is a sudden, discordant note trumpeted in my ear. Jillian has never said sorry about anything the entire time I've known her, and to hear it now—for the one thing she *didn't* actually do—sets my teeth on edge. "Just Elias, though, right?"

Jillian looks up from her delicate work to glare at me. "Is now really the time?"

"Considering our current predicament, I think it's the only time we might have."

She sets the scissors down with a hard click and starts wrapping one of the bandages diagonally from my chest around my good shoulder. "I was angry that night, yes, but I can't believe you thought I might shoot you."

"It was a perfectly logical leap when I thought you had sicced Interpol on me," I counter. "But I'm not talking about the bullet, Jill. I'm talking about the last three years. Was a bad lay really enough for you to ruin my whole damn life?"

Her hands pause right over my heart. "What?"

"You already had what you wanted. I left you alone, exactly like you asked for. Did you have to keep punishing me?"

Jillian withdraws from me in slow, jerky movements, folding into herself like a hibiscus facing the dark, narrow and withered. Rage wars with disbelief in her eyes. "You think this happened because we had sex? Really?"

What is that supposed to mean? "You haven't given me any other explanation. And trust me, I looked for one, every goddamn day."

"Your *note*, Sloane," she grits through clenched teeth. "You thought that's what I wanted? Are you trying to spin breaking my heart as a kindness?"

Breaking *her* heart? Maybe the gunshot actually killed me and I ended up in purgatory—or a mirror dimension. "I didn't think anything, Jillian. You told me you wanted to be alone. You didn't want a partner. You would never settle. Ever."

Her face pales. "That was before you. I let you in, and you abandoned me."

She's serious. So utterly convinced that I can't even think

past my shock for a solid minute. The only sound I can muster is a low, hollow laugh.

"You said so many things to me that night," I whisper. "A thousand promises, a thousand demands. And not once— not *once*—did you tell me to stay. You wouldn't have even had to say please. Just 'stay'. But you didn't. So I left first, before you could see the look on my face when I was doing it. I left the note so you would think I was just like you, that I didn't need anyone else. Because I couldn't fucking stand the thought of being kicked out. I'd have snapped in two."

"You were the exception to the rule!" The shine on hazel eyes is so strong, I realize she's a breath away from tears; I've never seen Jillian cry. "How did you not know? You read every person who meets you down to the marrow, Sloane, and you couldn't read me? I don't believe it."

"I'm not a telepath," I snap. "Everyone else is predictable. You're not. Was I supposed to rip apart every boundary you'd ever set on a whim? On a guess? Assuming I knew better than the woman who made it exceedingly clear she didn't need anyone else? I left that note for you to make *you* feel better."

Jillian chokes down a rough breath and drops her head into her hands. "Reading it killed a part of me. I waited days for you to take those words back, to say anything else, but there was nothing but silence."

My jaw drops. "Because I didn't—because if I looked clingy, I thought you'd never talk to me again. And instead of asking me what happened, you sicced another thief on me."

I never wanted to write the note. Every word killed a part of me too. If she asked, I would have shackled my entire life to her whim if it meant the occasional night of freedom, where I could be myself with the only person in the world who understood me. No matter what lies I had to tell. Even if she never gave me commitment.

"You started this," I hiss through my teeth. "And you could have stopped it at any time. You fucked me over for years because you couldn't spit out that you finally grew a heart and wanted someone else. Would it have ruined your reputation, jewel? Were you afraid that with the two of us on actually even ground, you'd lose?"

She looks up from the cradle of her hands. "Fuck you."

"Even now, you won't admit it." My chest burns, but the fire is spreading. "Say the words: 'stay, Sloane, stay.' You don't want me dead, but you don't want me close either. Tell the truth, Jill."

Her mouth opens then closes. Tears spill down the side of Jillian's face, and it feels like staring at stigmata, something no mortal should see. Guilt surges from the pit of my stomach, only to bolt at the heat conquering the rest of my body. I could blame the whisky, but the fact is, I've wanted to say this for years.

If she won't fill the silence, I will.

"Falling in love with you was the worst thing that's ever happened to me."

CHAPTER 17

JILLIAN

Sloane loved me.

I didn't see it, the same way I didn't see Elias was undercover. What else have I missed? What else have I burned to the ground to keep my life untethered, hiding gut-deep fear under a veneer of stoic independence? The note got so close to catching me, I set everything around it ablaze too, not caring if Sloane was scorched in the process.

They're not lying, no matter how much I want that to be true. I never asked them to stay. I simply wished a thousand times in my head when Sloane was touching me that they would read the plea on my skin, trapped and screaming in my heart. I wanted them to conquer that fear for me, to stake a claim I couldn't refuse. Saying yes would have been the easiest thing in the world, but asking the question without knowing the answer? I couldn't bear it. If Sloane had said no, my life would have crumbled to ash.

Hasn't it anyway?

Tears won't stop coming down my face. They're past the point of control, a scared animal reflex in the echo of an unimaginable mistake. Every move I make is meant to be five steps ahead, an equation to solve. I didn't just fail to take in account my own margin for error—I never considered Sloane wouldn't be able to see past my guise. Putting them on a pedestal primed them for a near-fatal fall.

"I'm sorry," I gasp—the second time in minutes, the second time in years. "I didn't think there was any chance you felt the same."

Sloane slides off the edge of the tub to marble tile with a hard thud, followed by an agonized curse. I reach for them, then recoil. Is it even right to offer comfort at this point?

"You felt the same?" Their question comes out as a wheeze. "Jillian..."

How could I not be in love with them? It would be like forcing the world not to spin. I've shared my bed too many times to count, but being with Sloane wasn't about that at all. If I didn't care, if I didn't want everything, the ache would have been gone in an instant. Instead, the need pierced through me like hate, wrapped in so much pain it was impossible to tell the difference.

"You could have anyone." I press down on the old, scarred wound around my heart, forcing the poison out. Every fear, every doubt. "I knew that. People smile the second you step into a room. They give up their fortunes. They fall for you. I think you could tell everyone you ever stole from what you did, and half of them would forgive you on the spot. I couldn't trust that... I hadn't just fallen into your orbit. Another target. Another mark."

They swallow hard. "I never turned the charm on you."

A bark of a laugh escapes my throat before I can stop it. "Oh? Then I was doomed from the start. I almost let you have everything the first night we met in person. I wanted to throw myself at you."

"It didn't show," Sloane mutters. "You're the real deal, you know. People talk about building themselves up from nothing, but you didn't have a mentor, or money, or a crew. Every theft was your plan from the ground up, stealing the impossible without anyone else to rely on. Whenever I found out where you were and what you were taking, I felt like an amateur. Nothing but flash."

"You were so confident." After wrangling back a sob, I wipe my face clean. "I didn't even care that you kept finding me. It should have been a risk, something to fear, but I loved it. The simple act of seeing you made me so damn happy."

"I..." Their face falls. "I'm sorry too. I did hurt you. I could have stopped the cycle at any time, but I was obsessed. I thought if I didn't strike back, I would lose the last connection I had to you. Anger was better than silence."

Jesus. We're unbelievably fucked.

This emotional folie à deux is enough on its own, but one of several federal agencies could have put that camera out in the hall, and even if Elias has only been tracking Sloane for a year, he's been tracking me five times longer. If Sloane is right about who is behind everything, no fewer than three blades of law enforcement are primed to skewer us from any given direction. I would have to be weightless, invisible, and able to walk through walls before getting away with taking Key's pictures in these circumstances.

Running wouldn't change much. Conspiracy charges don't require a criminal act to be completed, just that an attempt to subvert the law was made, and both Sloane and I are guilty of that in spades. Our determination to get in each other's way surely left behind evidence on its own, years of intersecting trails offering a clean highlight of our careers, blatant as the gold Klimt wrapped around *Judith*'s throat.

Stealing the photos now would be madness.

Then, Sloane leans forward, intent in their eyes, and sanity seems optional. A few scarce inches from me and they stall out, having to use their good arm to brace back against the tub, and I move without thinking, narrowing the gap between us on hands and knees.

"Stop hurting yourself for me," I say.

Sloane's knowing look has the same weight as their touch. "At this point, it's habit."

They're close enough to kiss, but I don't dare. I can't move on without getting one more answer, even if it means taking a slippery step on the tightrope hanging between us.

"I have a question to ask," I start, trying to ground myself with a palm against cool tile, hard and unbreakable. "You don't have to answer if you don't want to. It's not fair for me to demand the truth. But I'd hate myself for wasting a second chance after I demolished the first."

Tension pulls along Sloane's brow. "I'm listening."

"You said falling in love with me was the worst thing that ever happened to you." Their face blanks, stripped of emotion, but I can't stop now. Even if the first step forward is my last, fear won't win. Not this time. "Do you still love me? Is it in present tense?"

Wary, ice-cold and glass-fragile, Sloane asks, "Does that matter?"

"Right now, the way you feel matters to me more than anything else," I insist. "Yes or no, it matters. Vengeance is off the table. I'm a grown woman, and it's time I acted like it."

I decide to offer proof by finishing the pressure bandage around their chest, connecting the intersection of elastic with little steel clips from the kit. Sloane's silence is imposing, but I weather the quiet without expectation.

Assuming and predicting is exactly how we got into this mess in the first place.

"Of course it's in the present tense, Jillian Rhodes," Sloane finally whispers. They look utterly exposed, naked and defiant as Cabanel's fallen angel. "Have you met you? You're impossible. You're everything I want, everything I *need* in one incomparable package. So if I'm alone, tell me now. Cut the damn tether."

I can't. The blade might as well be pointed at my throat.

"I love you too." A dam breaks in my chest. I choke back a sob, trying to stop a fresh flood of tears. Faced with the absurd rush of what we've done to each other, another confession slips through: "And you're fantastic in bed."

Sloane cracks a grin, empty of feeling. "You don't have to soothe my ego."

"That night was the only time I ever lied to you." I hold up my hand so they can see the still-healing crescents in my palm. "I used the oldest trick in the book."

They stare at me for a solid ten seconds before their shoulders start to shake with laughter. Sloane's head bows, but when they look back up, their smile is real and vicious with delight.

"You're lucky I'm injured right now," they say, "or you would be in so much trouble."

Liquid heat infuses Sloane's voice; I shiver. "Is that so?"

"Mm*hmm*." They roll the second syllable like they're picturing exactly how I would fit in their mouth. "I'd spank you red, girl."

The good news is that my anxiety instantly evaporates due to the surge of lust pulsing through my body. The bad news is I need blood back in my brain to think of how to get Sloane and I out of this mess.

"Rain check?" I ask breathlessly.

Sloane nods, leashing their desire. Ever the professional. "You look scared, Jill."

"I'm terrified. I want you so much, I feel like I'm going to crush you trying to reach for it." More poison, more honesty, dripping out in a steady stream. "Except we're surrounded. They may not be breaking down your door now, but they will soon. We're on a deadline. Steal or run. Lose either way."

"You never take a challenge lying down," they say.

No, never. Which is why I have to do this.

"I'm going to take Key's pictures exactly when they expect it. And you'll be on a plane somewhere, anywhere else. If they catch me, then they catch me, but I'll never give them your name. I don't care what they offer me."

"Fuck's sake." Sloane laughs again, and the sound clashes with the tension holding my chest in a vise, dividing it in two. "If you think I'm letting you take the fall by yourself, you don't know me at all."

"I'm the one who started this—"

Their expression turns stone serious. "Every time you lashed out, I struck back, Jill. I brigaded you over some pretty terrible shit. I'm no saint here. I have no idea what you and I will look like after this, but I am sure as hell not saving my own skin at your expense."

If they're with me, maybe there's a chance. A sliver of a chance, dependent on so many factors a single pin slipping out of alignment could condemn the rest. There's not enough smoke and mirrors in the world to cover Sloane's and my tracks, but there might be enough to turn our pursuers on each other.

"I have a plan," I say. "But if it doesn't work, we'll be in ten times the trouble we are now."

Sloane smiles. "I'm in."

"You haven't even heard the plan yet."

Their asymmetrical shrug is equal parts dismissive and attractive. "Like I said, I'm in."

"But if—"

"Jillian. Jewel. Queen of thieves." The tips of my ears burn red. That's a new one. "If you're planning the take, I'm for it. Just tell me what we need."

I take a deep breath. Time to dive. Time to fall.

"What do you know about light exposure techniques?"

CHAPTER 18
SLOANE

T arrive at the Institute with a minute to spare.
Chicago socialites form a golden host at the front
of the museum, directed in ones and twos through a
tunnel of glass doors, permanently propped open for the
evening. Despite half the city's GDP walking around on
display, press is scarce; I expect Clayton promised a scoop to
the *Tribune* tomorrow morning in order to keep the third-
shift reporters from biting at the ankles of every donor in
proximity.

The lead docent by the door has a tablet in hand,
marking off names rather than checking tickets or barcodes
on phones. Everyone with a Luminary title expects to be
known by virtue of their presence, a frictionless dominance
only the wealthy can demand. To the docent's credit, he
seems to know almost everyone personally, delivering spiels
on seat location and vegetarian preference without ever
looking down at his screen.

"Sloane Caffrey?" When I nod, his professional veneer
stretches out to a smile before relaxing again. He'll do it a

hundred more times tonight—I sure hope the Institute pays well. "Welcome to the Premiere Luminary gala. Is your plus one with you?"

"She's running a little late." I offer my own smile, conspiratorial enough to amuse him. "Can she get in without me, or should I come back to the door?"

"I'll make sure she's directed to your table." He taps the screen twice, highlighting my name in green, and an answering square lights up on the map of the interior. "Which is number seven. A bartender is on staff to create anything you like."

Just like that, I'm inside. The usual security booth has been pulled out of the way, hidden behind the day ticket line by a weave of velvet ropes. Fifty tables have taken over the open marble lobby, draped with red cloth rich enough to hide spilled wine and liquor, gold thread decorating the edges for a bit of flair. I can only imagine what Kruger would think about *I shop therefore I am* hanging over such an abject display of consumerism, turning the public display of art into private, consumptive indulgence.

Ella is already at number seven, her phone in one hand and a glass of champagne in the other. She looks up when I approach, then blinks twice. "Okay, I'm impressed. Much better than a tux."

I settled on a Dormeuil Vanquish II in deep forest green, offset against my eyes. Most nights I eschew ties, but a six-centimeter wide silk blade dripping with jade pendants is the kind of statement piece unsuitable for almost any other occasion. My cufflinks match the stones, cradled in silver crowns. I would have worn earrings to match, but not on a night the cops might shove my face to the floor. Regardless, I'm a pickpocket's wet dream, walking around with wealth like armor, artifice masquerading as protection.

No keys are in my pockets, whether to pick open cuffs or slip through the elevator. I have no weapons, and my ruined bulletproof vest was disposed of back at the Peninsula. My wallet holds the bare necessities of legal ID, accurate and up to date, not a single falsehood among them. Even the barest suggestion of criminality could condemn me here, which meant leaving behind the Rolodex of potential saviors in my personal cell phone. I made a single call before leaving the hotel, locked the phone in a lead case, then put that case in the room safe.

A burner weighs down my other pocket with enough credit for a handful of texts, and it won't survive the night. Everything is disposable; I'm bait for a single devastating hook.

Jillian entered the Institute three hours ago, and so far, no one seems any the wiser.

"Come on, sit." Ella gestures to the seat next to her. "Don't bother going over to the bar for drinks. The staff Dad hired comes around every thirty seconds to make sure no one's holding an empty glass."

"Thanks." I sit down and gesture at her phone. "Texting with Joana?"

She clears her throat, looking like I've just caught her walking off with a sculpture from one of the exhibits next door. "Texting. Calling. Video chatting. I feel like I'm in high school again, crushing on the hottest girl in the class, except the girl is actually into me? You have good taste in women, Sloane, even if their taste isn't you."

"Can't win them all," I joke. "Besides, history has proven I can only handle one woman at a time, max."

Intrigue puts a warm glint in brown eyes. "Oh? Is there one who got away?"

Jillian did get away, but now she's within my reach again.

She's in love with me.

The knowledge floats around me, adrift as ink atop water. If look too closely or try to catch the truth in my hands, it will break apart into a thousand little spirals, never to reform again. I was so sure she hated me, facing the truth seems like a trick.

Belated honesty can't cure the last three years, much as I want it to. For so long, the angry pressure in my heart triumphed, held open like a surgeon's balloon trying to save a vital artery from withering. The valve has burst, the pain is gone, but scar tissue has formed around the hollow, memorializing the damage.

I don't hate her. The exact opposite, in fact. But I'm drowning in guilt.

If I had told Jillian about Elias when I was arrested, we wouldn't be here now. Except I convinced myself she had to know, that there was no way a cop could flit in and out of her life without immediately attracting attention. One assertion fed into another—if she knew about Elias, she sent him after me on purpose—building a Tower of Babel, miscommunication fueling rage. I never considered Jillian could make a mistake.

No one's perfect. Casting her as an infallible mastermind made her beyond human, an unfeeling force of nature battering my life on a whim. When I stopped treating her as a person, I forgot she could feel, that she could hurt as deeply as I do. Jillian and I were fighting illusions of each other, waging war ten steps ahead of our predictions instead of facing our fears in the present.

I want to wade into the wreckage, to try and salvage

what we had, but that means surviving tonight. So I can't afford to get distracted.

"Kind of. She keeps me humble," I say to Ella, calling up a smile. "If I don't bend the knee once in a while, I turn intolerable."

She laughs before we're interrupted by one of the ever-present staff. I order a straight vodka, then watch as the server weaves back through the crowd. Three pairs of eyes trace the path between us—feds. Agents aren't difficult to find once you know what you're looking for. Some superior or another bullied them into getting their tuxedos tailored, but the giveaway is in the shoes. They're far too cheap for a gala like this, tactically flat and the same dim black as their jackets.

The burner in my pocket buzzes with a text. It's a chain of numbers and letters —*DOB05131967LOC34.5199N105.8701W*—broken into lines to look like spam, but rife with information I need. After turning off the phone, I pocket it again and use my thumb to rip out the battery. The SIM card comes next. Three different garbage cans are on the way to Contemporary Art; I'll dispose of each piece separately.

My drink arrives, and right as the glass is offered to me, the lights go out. I yank it out of the server's hand, directing the vodka to spill across my jacket. In the dark, someone screams. Another voice—the docent from the door—calls for everyone to be calm, and the lights blink back to life.

The federal trio is half a room closer to me than they were a moment before, looking puzzled to a man that I didn't leave my seat.

"I'm so sorry," the server starts. She's young, inexperienced, and calculating how much my tie costs in comparison to her entire net worth. "I'll get some napkins—"

"Don't worry about it." I give Ella an apologetic look. "I need five minutes to clean this up. Mind if I leave you alone?"

After a quick glance at her phone, she grins. "If Joana keeps texting me like this, I might *oblige* you to leave me alone."

Good. I need her preoccupied.

One bad tux tracks me with his eyes when I head towards the bathroom but doesn't follow any further. After I'm beyond his line of sight, I dispose of the burner bit by bit in each garbage can. Not a foolproof method, but the more resources I can get a forensics team to waste, the better.

The gender-neutral restroom has its own door with a lock. I step inside and promptly close it behind me. When I flip on the lights, I'm treated to the sublime view of Jillian's bare back as she steps into her dress, which doesn't cover an inch above the curve of her hips. It's a tight black number with thin straps around the shoulders, so very easy to tug aside, framing the rest of her body with promise. The graceful line of her throat is left open, pale and unmarked.

Before I can start to actively fantasize, she turns around to scan me up and down.

"What was your poison?"

"Vodka," I say. "Dries odorless and colorless."

I use a paper towel to dab at the worst of the stain anyway, trying to keep my heart rate under control at the sight of the drab brown envelope balanced on top of the trash can. Out of their top-shelf cases, Key's prints are remarkably small.

"You look good," Jillian notes, daring to smile.

"So do you."

My heart might be ground down to paste, but with

Jillian, my libido has an instant override—one hot, blood-heavy path cleaving through everything else. Thankfully, my brain uses executive veto and reminds the other organs involved we won't be getting anywhere facing several decades in prison.

"The guards in the vault didn't seem to recognize me," she notes, then gestures to the garbage. "I had to toss the wig here. Flushed the contacts. Changed my makeup. So now we just need to get out intact."

"Three feds are watching gala-side. You'll have to pass them to get back around to the front and make your entrance."

Jillian picks up the envelope. "Want a look inside first?"

It could be empty. She might be setting me up for one hell of a fall, and at this point nothing would change the outcome. But despite every screaming self-preservation instinct, I want to trust her. "No thanks. I just spent sixteen hours staring at those pictures."

"True." She tucks the photos into the wide belly of her purse and then clicks it shut. "Block the feds as I head out. I'll cut through Greco-Roman Antiquities and meet you by the docent in two minutes."

In this line of work, two minutes is a damn long time. "Let's go."

I'm already counting seconds as we leave the bathroom, calculating sight angles and reaction time as the first ill-heeled fed catches sight of me again. Jillian knows my steps, but I have to bet she can walk in my shadow without ever looking back to check. I cut a half-circle through the gala where the crowd is thickest, cross my fingers, and drift back towards Ella.

No alarm rings out. The boys in the suits don't come running.

"I have to go give your father a very large check," I tell Ella, who has gone through another glass of champagne in my absence. "Our deal is done, so I hope you enjoy the rest of the evening."

She smiles. "You fake date better than most of my real dates. Enjoy your plaque, Sloane."

Oh, I will.

Ella pays no mind as I bypass our table for the docent, right as Jillian walks up to the front of the Institute. He checks her in without concern, and I silently match her step for step as we make our way towards the Contemporary Art wing, dressed to kill and with nothing to hide.

Tension unfurls in my chest. She stayed.

Two steps from the velvet rope, they rush us. Someone's hard grip yanks my arms back before handcuffs lock around both wrists, a low federal drawl breathing hot against my ear.

"Sloane Caffrey and Jillian Rhodes, you are under arrest for six counts of theft of a major artwork, second-degree burglary, criminal impersonation, and conspiracy to commit fraud. You have the right to remain silent. Anything you say can and will be used against you in a court of law—"

One last roll of the dice is coming, Jill.

Don't lose faith in me now.

CHAPTER 19

JILLIAN

The feds march me and Sloane through a pitch-black hallway into the Contemporary Art wing, opening up into the light of Key's gallery. Every locked frame is a blank slate, wide white squares surrounded by glass and wide granite bases.

Our escort is silent, but they're not the main event. The stars of the evening are waiting in front of open glass doors: Director Clayton Woodward, Elias—go fuck yourself, *cop*—Denning, and a woman I've never met before. I suppose pickpocketing her an hour ago might count as an introduction, but I returned her wallet after getting the information I needed, so who's to say?

Assistant Special Agent in Charge—FBI titles are a ridiculous mouthful—Lydia Walker has only two inches of height on me, but her aura of command stretches a mile in every direction. Dark brown hair curls down her shoulders, and the faint warmth of sun-drenched skin is sapped by the shards of ice in shocking blue eyes. She's pressing into her fifties, but clever makeup downplays about a decade, smoothing her face and sharpening her jaw.

Elias tries to meet my gaze, but I refuse him the pleasure. Priority one is Sloane and me getting out of this with our freedom intact; leaving his career in a smoking crater comes in a very close second.

"Jillian—" he starts.

I keep my eyes on Walker. "Do I know you?"

"This isn't the time to play games, Ms. Rhodes," she counters. Her familiar alto tone holds a keen weight, used to dominating a room—or a rooftop.

"The FBI seems to be the one playing games," Sloane chimes in. "Because this is a very interesting choice of interrogation room."

"This is a crime scene." Walker gestures back to the gallery. The other agents have fallen around her in a half-circle, standing at attention. They can see her, but not any further inside. Good enough. "Russell Key's photos were stolen less than an hour ago, but as far as we can tell, the pictures haven't left the museum. The agency has a wealth of evidence confirming the two of you were responsible, so if you'd like to make your lives any easier, now is the time."

If they had evidence, we would already be in the back of a black van.

"I'm afraid I have no idea what you're talking about," Sloane says, annoyance creasing their brow. "I came here to give Director Woodward a check."

Lights—

I press down against the inside of my right heel, wedging my stockinged foot against the device hiding in the toe. The button depresses, and every lit bulb in the gallery goes out for the second time tonight. In the span of five seconds, my arresting agent has snared me in a bruising grip, half a dozen bodies move towards us in the dark, and I hear a sharp, telling click.

Camera—

When the gallery illuminates itself again, the previously composed circle of agents is trapped mid-chaos, two of them guarding Woodward while the rest tried to swarm Sloane and myself. Elias' jacket is mussed from an unexpected collision, which would make me smile, but the most important tell comes from Walker.

Her hand is on her gun—an M&P Shield—and it's halfway out of the holster, safety flicked off from a burst of well-honed reflex. Anger brews on Walker's face as her hand relaxes, letting go of the weapon in perfect silence.

—Action. Three minutes and counting.

"Was that your idea of an escape plan?" she asks, mockery slicing through her tone.

"No." Sloane's voice raises their voice, an open challenge to Walker's air of command. "But you're quite fast on the draw... Adriana."

She's good. Surprise stays muted around her eyes and mouth, a blink suppressed, the urge to lick her lips pulled back to a faint purse. Elias, however, can't help himself. He laughs, giving Sloane a wry look.

"I think you have a case of mistaken identity. Agent Walker isn't—"

"In 1990, it was Adriana Azevedo. Miss Rio de Janeiro." Sloane continues, as if Elias hadn't spoken at all. "Which is interesting because Agent Walker isn't Brazilian. She was born and raised in New Mexico in 1967. You must have done very well in your Portuguese classes at Camp Peary."

"You *do* have the right to remain silent, Mx. Caffrey," Walker says. "I highly recommend you use it before opening your mouth again."

"Peary?" Elias scoffs. "She's FBI, not CIA."

Walker's jaw tenses. I'm sure she wishes Elias would exercise the same right, but I knew he wouldn't. Even if I missed his true loyalties, I still read him correctly as a person: desperate to be the center of attention, a glory hound, the kind of man who raises his hand before he even knows the answer, hoping to be chosen first.

"She's both," Sloane declares plainly. "Although a lot's changed. You don't straighten your hair anymore, Agent. Stopped going to the tanning booth and waxing yourself into a model Barbie doll. Thirty plus years reshapes everyone, but one thing doesn't change. Your eyes can still make a whole room stop in place."

Walker sneers. "You have one hell of an imagination."

"Do I? I'm sure it wasn't hard for the Agency to bribe some judges and help you win a few beauty contests simply by showing up. Once you had the title, that was enough notoriety to get Russell Key's attention. He ate fame for breakfast. You were young—younger than him, so he'd never be suspicious—and too beautiful to resist. The perfect honeypot to trap a man funding a rebirth of the same pesky student rebel groups the CIA quashed in the sixties."

Elias' wary gaze drifts toward Walker. This is Sloane's true gift, fascinating an entire room with their words, even when the audience has every reason to believe they're a liar. Their voice is a lure, too bright not to chase, too stunning to ever capture.

"And you disappeared just as easily. The whole country saw the two of you together. Russell had a reputation as a coke fiend. Him murdering his pretty girlfriend in a fit of passion was a simple sell to every local rag hunting for a headline. You didn't even bother leaving a body behind.

Bribing cops back then cost, what, a hundred cruzado? Pocket change."

Two minutes.

"You knew he had taken pictures of you both. Explicit ones. But he was going to be arrested, his belongings swept up as evidence. Easy enough to dispose of the proof, kill the alias, then move onto your next job. Except your fellow agents couldn't find the photos, could they? And you couldn't show your face in Brazil for a good long while. After a year, you probably told yourself they were lost. After ten, surely they were gone. Then Key died, and his old Rio landlord turned that apartment upside down. Nice guy, sending the pictures back to Key's wife instead of selling them off himself."

"If you have a point, get to it," Walker snaps.

"You can take over any time," Sloane replies with a smile. "If I'm getting the details wrong, just say the word."

Her silence, no matter how cold, is beyond satisfying.

"The question is, how did you find out where the pictures were sent? Marisa Key certainly didn't want her husband's affair publicized. But then I realized, you were keeping surveillance on the family the entire time, weren't you? When you heard the news on whatever bug was collecting dust in their house, you needed someone to take the photos for you. A case with a *legal* warrant could have seized them as evidence, but the CIA never found out about your screw-up, did they? And the FBI certainly didn't know when you took a lateral promotion into their ranks."

Director Woodward is starting to sweat through his shirt. "Agent Walker, is any of this true? This is—"

She cuts him off with a glare. "Irrelevant."

"It isn't irrelevant." His brows tense. "Rondeaux told me the Institute had a standing relationship with you. That we

RIEN GRAY

were legally obliged to keep the photos in our vault out of harm's way. Then suddenly, you tell me to put them on display."

And then an anonymous note arrived on Russell Key Jr's doorstep warning that his father's photos were about to be shown to the rest of the world. I gave him a call this morning —he was just as surprised to hear from me again as he was to find out the CIA was spying on his house, and twice as angry to find out the woman responsible was the same one who slept with dear old Dad in the first place.

"But you didn't actually want this collection to go public," Sloane adds, "so the pictures had to become evidence in another case. An indisputable crime that would allow the FBI to seize everything and walk out the door untouched."

One minute and counting.

"You needed a thief," I say, finally looking Elias in the eye. "But just to be sure, you decided to pick two."

He chuckles, dry with disbelief. "Is that a confession? Because we have video of you going into the kid's house."

"I'm just an appraiser," I say. "If the photos were confirmed to be legitimate, I would have helped him sue the Institute for custody."

"Bullshit." Elias shakes his head. "There's no getting out of this. I've seen you work for years."

"Then I'm sure there's recorded evidence of that too, isn't there?" I raise a brow. "Please, Elias. Enlighten me."

His sallow face pales even further. With a short crop of brown hair in desperate need of styling, it gives him the look of a sickly mouse. "You always searched me for a wire. You had a white noise app on your phone so the bugs couldn't pick anything up."

"Did I? How shrewd." Maybe I didn't sense Elias was a

156

cop because he's such an impotent one. "When you put it that way, it really seems like your word against mine."

"*Enough*," Walker growls. "The only way either of you could have figured any of this out is if you planned to steal the photographs. Motive is clear as day."

"Actually, I found out by going on a date with his daughter." Sloane gestures with a tilt of their head towards Woodward. "She made the lovely display right behind me about the murder case and its controversy."

The other agents stare at the massive media spread behind Sloane, who remains in the spotlight with a serene look on their face. Walker could challenge them at any time, claim she found Sloane trying to climb onto the museum's roof, but that would mean admitting she shot them unprovoked.

"There's also one little problem." Sloane leans in, and I hold my breath. Five. Four. "I didn't steal any pictures." Three. Two. "And I don't think Jillian did either, considering they're sitting in those *very* secure frames inside the gallery."

One.

The whole room freezes. Dread cracks Walker's mask of authority as she slowly turns on one heel, looking through the open doors.

Every frame holds a beautiful photograph—Key's work down to the last detail. Director Woodward sputters, looking between us and the gallery no less than three times before finally managing to gasp, "I... What the hell is going on here?"

"That *is* you," Elias mutters, staring at the first picture front and center, where 'Adriana' stands naked with Key. "Oh my God."

"Shut up," Walker spits out. "Director, give me the camera feed for the last hour. That's an order."

"You do not order me around, ma'am." His back straightens, steel stiff. "And it wouldn't matter if I got you the feed. Our cameras aren't pointed at the pictures."

She blinks. "What?"

"They're pointed at the guests. You can't keep a camera directly above any display. If the wiring goes awry or a battery leaks acid, it can destroy priceless works of art."

Walker pinches a tight line of tension between her brows and scoffs. "Then get me *those* recordings."

They won't find anything. A camera has several advantages over the human eye yet falls to plenty of tricks we can see right through. I rolled the aperture of mirrors—presently ten feet away from Agent Walker—inside the gallery to access the frames. The reflective surface projected a copy of the room back to the cameras, and its heavy glass body kept the heat of mine from setting off the motion detectors. With Sloane's copy of the magnetic key, I stood in the camera's blind spot and opened every case, taking the photos for myself and secreting them away. A ghost in all but name.

Replacing them with the fakes was even easier because Sloane is unmatched when it comes to forgery. They recreated Key's work from max resolution pictures on their phone and photochromic ink, which responds when properly exposed to light. One exposure turns everything pure white—the second brings back the image in a little under three minutes.

"Um, ma'am?" One of the FBI agents steps forward, a phone to his ear. "There's a lawyer outside for the suspects. She's very insistent."

Good timing. I was just starting to get tired of these cuffs.

CHAPTER 20

SLOANE

K imberly steps into the gallery with the imposing air of a queen.

In terms of law, she may as well be one. Her arguments have made it to the Supreme Court—twice—and she presently sits on the board of the National Law Review, which just so happens to be based in Chicago. Kimberly keeps an office in San Francisco, but her influence has an international profile, which is how she freed me from Spanish lockup while several time zones away.

She must have put half the gala to shame walking inside too. A warm emerald Jason Wu dress with a clever drape twisted up and around Kimberly's throat is offset with a Serpenti purse and matching bracelets, blending galuchat with malachite as black-and-white enamel snake heads declare a warning to anyone in her proximity.

Anyone would be forgiven for missing Russell Key Jr. in her shadow, especially when he shuffles half a step behind the hard click of Kimberly's three-inch heels. He didn't bother to dress up, both hands shoved into the pockets of a worn sheepskin jacket I glimpsed in one of his father's photos. They really are a spitting image of each other, which works to my advantage.

I want Lydia Walker to look him in the eyes.

"This is a closed scene," she says. "Get them out of here."

"I have a right to a lawyer since you put these on me." I shrug, tugging at the slender chain of the handcuffs. "And if anyone can verify the veracity of the gallery's photos, it's Key's son. Unless you have a reason why he shouldn't be allowed to see them."

"This is an active criminal investigation." Lydia's eyes narrow. "I can keep out whoever I want."

"Do your FBI superiors know you're in those pictures?" Jillian asks. "Or did you only share secrets with your CIA friends stalking around the roof the other night? I'd love to know if that was a sanctioned operation."

A couple of the agents near her suddenly look very uncomfortable. Elias in particular is flabbergasted, pacing a line back and forth in front of the gallery doors.

"Adriana," he starts, then roughly clears his throat. "Sorry. I mean, Lydia—"

If looks could kill, her glare would put Elias six feet under. "That's Agent Walker to you, Denning."

"Agent Walker, I have to know that this case is on the up-and-up. If these arrests get thrown out, Interpol will have my head. We already cut a deal with one informant."

I have a very good suspicion about who that informant is.

"Ma'am, I think we should—" another agent begins.

"Everyone close your mouths for half a damn minute!" Walker bellows.

In the gap of silence, Kimberly steps into the light of the gallery, one brow raised. "And here I thought the party was in the other room. Although it's looking a bit more like a circus." Dark brown eyes meet mine. "You get into the most interesting sort of trouble, Sloane."

She's immune to my charm, but that doesn't stop me from smiling. "Not through any fault of my own."

Clayton gives me a harried look. "I'm sorry about all of this. The evidence she gave me—and you had access—"

"Because they *did*," Walker interrupts. "Both of them. The pictures were missing, Director. Everyone in this room saw the empty frames."

"Really?" I ask. "Because I can't recall."

Rage flashes across her face. If we weren't in a room full of people, I'm pretty sure she would shoot me a second time. "I don't know what trick you and your girlfriend pulled, but you won't get away with it."

"Do you hear that, Jill?" I glance her way. "We're dating."

She chuckles. "Lucky us."

"You hate them," Elias sputters. "Jillian, you told me that. The two of you had been after each other for years. How..."

"Seems like you got your hands on some bad intel, Denning." She doesn't bother keeping the ice out of her voice. "Because this entire thing feels like entrapment. You can't catch Sloane on some trumped-up charge, so you what, set both of us up instead? I'm going to sue you until your grandchildren are in debt."

"And she has quite the case," Kimberly adds. "Because in my view, this is a gross miscarriage of justice, as well as substantial overreach by the federal government, if not outright fraud on your part, Agent Walker."

"The pictures were gone!" Walker laughs, bitter with disbelief. "I have an entire room of witnesses."

"But no actual proof," I note. "So you can't make a case

for sweeping the photos into evidence. The exhibit can go off without a hitch tomorrow."

"*No.*" The control around her voice wears thin. "I'm filing an injunction with a judge tonight. If you put those photos on display, Director, you'll be held in contempt."

"You have no claim to make," Clayton protests. "The pictures are right here, and I'm certainly not lying on your behalf. Not again."

Walker works her tongue against her teeth, jaw tight. "I have probable cause to believe these pictures violate the Intelligence Identities Protection Act."

"Your identity!" He shakes his head, overwhelmed. "This is unbelievable. Twenty billion dollars worth of equity is standing in the other room waiting for this announcement, Agent. If I have nothing to show them, this museum will go bankrupt."

"And that's your problem, isn't it?" Harsh blue eyes lock onto Russell Key Jr. "Confirm those pictures are real. Then I'm taking them into evidence. I will arrest anyone who tries to interfere, and you will not like where I put you afterwards."

Russell looks to Kimberly, who nods. I stay idle with Jillian as he walks past us, showing no sign of recognition.

"He hired her to steal them," Elias mutters under his breath. "You can't just..."

"Go back to Lyon, Denning," Walker says. "Interpol has used enough of the Bureau's resources already."

"But you—" He puts a hand over his face. "I'm so screwed."

"Couldn't have happened to a nicer person," Jillian says.

Elias is too devastated to have a quip in kind. I watch him scurry out of the gallery, a rat to the very end, and bite back a laugh. Jill must be having the time of her life.

"They're real," Russell announces a few minutes later. "These are the same pictures the Institute took from my mom."

"Then you'll remove the handcuffs from my clients, posthaste." Kimberly levels Walker with a hard look, statuesque and immovable. "There was no theft, no burglary, and no basis for either an impersonation or fraud charge."

"Caffrey promised the Institute five million dollars to gain access to these pictures," Walker counters. "They never paid up."

I smile. "The check's in my jacket, agent. I just can't reach it at the moment."

Her jaw drops an inch before Walker recovers and sneers, "Fine. Get the cuffs off both of them."

Once my wrists are free, I pull out the check in question, offering it to Clayton. "I know it's a drop in the bucket in comparison, but I hope it will help."

"It will." His mouth tenses into a thin line. "I apologize for doubting you, Sloane."

Eventually the FBI will figure out the pictures are forgeries, but by then, Clayton will be out of the range of any splash damage. Admitting they were tricked twice would burn any shred of credibility Walker has left. "No need. I just have one of those faces. People think I'm capable of anything."

Jillian makes a quiet, choked sound from behind me but recovers by clearing her throat. "So, we're free to go?"

"Yes," Walker mutters. "Get out of my sight."

As the agents sweep into the gallery to take custody of the pictures, Russell steps back out, returning to the protective circle around Kimberly.

Jillian sidles up to Clayton and drops her voice to a whisper. "You know, every museum I've ever been to, some of their most famous pieces are sitting in storage. If you showed something off that no one else has, that your guests have never seen, the night might still be saved."

He frowns deeply. "Key's work had the appeal we were looking for. Sexuality, fame, murder. These days, you need all three to survive more than thirty seconds in the news."

"You wouldn't happen to have an Egon Schiele lying around, would you?" I bite my tongue trying not to smile; Jillian saw the piece herself while infiltrating the vault. "Horrible man. Dead at twenty-eight. Painted a ludicrous amount of pornography. And there isn't a single museum in the world right now that's bold enough to put his work on display."

"We have... two, actually." Clayton's shoulders straighten, his entire posture turning energetic. "I can show them at the gala in temporary frames, then tomorrow morning we can—God, we'll have to redo this gallery from scratch. We'll be paying double overtime."

"You have five million to spare," I say.

"Your plaque will be right in front," he insists, then sighs. "And it was a pleasure to meet you, Ms. Rhodes. Despite the circumstances."

Jillian follows me out of the gallery, shadowed by Kimberly and Russell. The gala is still in full swing, guests too occupied with liquor and one another to notice as our little pack leaves the Institute. I make a beeline for the set of benches on the edge of Millennium Park and reach underneath the concrete, prying free the envelope taped in place there.

Russell's eyes widen when I offer it to him. "You two really did it."

"And the fake collection we left behind stays under wraps," I say. "Thanks to Walker."

164

"Are you still going to burn the real ones?" Jillian asks.

He goes quiet with consideration for a long moment, turning the envelope back and forth in his hands. "Part of me wants to, just to be done with this. But the rest wants insurance in case the CIA ever wiretaps my house again."

Jillian gives his shoulder a light pat. "You did a good job keeping calm. And having a weapon on hand against a woman like Walker? Smart idea."

Russell nods. "You know, Dad told me a bunch of times he had been framed. I was so pissed at him about the affairs, I didn't believe it. Guess he wasn't paranoid, huh?"

"In your defense," I say, "the man did an inconceivable amount of cocaine."

He laughs then shakes his head. "Yeah, okay. True. But thank you. I need to get home so I can meet the tech you said would clean the bugs out."

"I'll drive him back to the airport." Kimberly looks me up and down. "Keep your nose clean for a little while, Sloane. You've already stolen a few hours of my beauty sleep."

"And you have my deepest apologies for that." She can pay for a full spa treatment out of my retainer. "I'll be good."

She gives my arm an affectionate squeeze before heading off with Russell, which leaves me alone in the shadows with Jillian. Wind whips through the park, and she shivers, wrapping both arms around herself before looking at me.

"We did it," Jillian says quietly. "Tipped the dominos back their way."

"Denning might even get fired," I add. "I can't believe he was onto you for that long and didn't get a single recording."

"Well, he's useless." She laughs, but the humor doesn't reach her eyes. "I... I know one night doesn't make up for everything I did, Sloane. There's so much old debris between us, I have no idea how to start clearing it away."

Me either. Burying myself in that old pain is easy as breathing, but it isn't what I want. Tonight was proof that we're made for each other, that even with the worst odds, Jillian and I can come out on top against the world. If she loves me—and I love her, down to my bones—then anything in our way deserves to burn.

"We could go clean slate. No looking back."

Hope flickers through her expression, a small and desperate spark. "Can we?"

I shrug. "Think of it like another job."

"Oh? What are we stealing now?"

"Three years of lost time."

Jillian's breath catches, her lips subtly parting. "Three years isn't enough. If we do this, you'll never get rid of me."

"That's the plan, jewel."

I'm not sure which one of us moves first, but her mouth is suddenly on mine, hot and wanting. I branded the memory of our last time together into the deepest part of my mind, but it's a pale illusion compared to the real thing, soft heat sinking into me as Jillian grabs the knot of my tie to keep me close. Her tongue sweeps my lip, and when I tease with my teeth in turn, a shiver goes through her body from head to toe.

She's my ruin and my greatest treasure, worth every risk and near miss. We can build something new, something better, from the ashes together. I kiss the promise into Jillian's skin, reveling in her shocked laugh when I lift her right off her feet. Lithe legs wrap around my waist, pressing her body against mine before hazel eyes widen.

"Shit, Sloane, your shoulder—"

"This is my good arm." I emphasize with a squeeze against her back.

"Where are you taking us?" she asks.

I smile. "You're going to have to trust me."

"With my whole heart, Sloane Caffrey." The warm amber of her eyes is so close, unguarded. After so long, she's finally showing me everything. "Keep it safe."

For the rest of my life—and then some.

CHAPTER 21

JILLIAN

We get a new hotel reservation in another city and a very different country.

The location is safe and anonymous, hidden under several layers of our respective aliases, in case our ruse with Walker unravels faster than expected. The high from screwing over both her and Elias still beats hot in my blood hours later as I walk into a room with subdued lights and cool sheets. Luxury lines every square inch of the place, waiting for reverence, but I can't keep my eyes off Sloane.

Where do I even begin? Our first time was a pressure cooker of desire hitting a boiling point, desire overwhelming sense, any notion of the future. That night, I tried to claw my need into their skin, as if a dozen red sigils would spell out the words I couldn't bear to say. I gorged on hunger and hope, only to be left starving the morning after. But I wanted to keep Sloane; I wanted them to love me.

Now that I know they do, now that I have them right in front of me, I'm terrified of destroying the fragile trust between us. Instinct tells me to bury the feeling, but I can't fall into that trap again—I won't.

"I'm nervous," I admit, breathless. "This feels like more of a first time than before."

"It does." In the half-light through the hotel window, Sloane is bisected by shadow. Their tie is long gone, jacket abandoned on the hook by the door, drawing my eyes to the bare triangle of skin between open buttons. "But I was nervous that night too. I thought it might be the only chance I ever got to touch you."

What am I waiting for? I want to banish that fear right out of their head.

Without my heels, I have to pull Sloane down to kiss them, but they bend without resistance, welcoming my mouth. Soft linen wrinkles under my fingertips as I grip tighter, never wanting to let go again. I shiver as their fingertips slip down the nape of my neck and fall even lower, caressing the bare length of my back. Light as touching glass, care and worship written into a single stroke. So damn gentle, my heart almost can't bear it.

"You can touch me wherever you want," I gasp against their mouth. "As long as you want. Don't hold back on me now."

"Then I need you horizontal." Their voice tilts lower, deep with promise, drawing out a well of heat between my thighs. "Because everything I plan to do is going to make your knees weak."

The hold around me tightens, and suddenly Sloane is in control, pushing me towards the bed. I know this dance, trading steps with them until the backs of my thighs meet the pale comforter. Their subtle push takes my balance, leaving me spread out across a white flag of surrender. When Sloane straddles me, knees framing my hips with warm weight, I can only watch as they strip the braid out of their hair, unfurling a curtain of red down their shoulders.

"It's cute when you play delicate," they say, leaning down to kiss me again. I answer with a bite to Sloane's lower lip. "I know you could throw me off this bed if you wanted to."

"*If* I wanted to," I mutter against their mouth. "It's more fun when you don't see it coming."

Their laugh is a caress of its own, breath spilling hot along the curve of my jaw. Sloane kisses around my pulse until it quickens, followed by a sharp graze of teeth down to my collarbone. I gasp, clutching at their shoulders, and a finger hooks under the strap of my dress, drawing the black fabric taut.

"I'm half-tempted to leave this tease of a dress on," they whisper, only to tug it down anyway, kissing over the skin they've just exposed, "but I want you naked under me more. I wonder how wet you'll be by the time I rip your panties off —if you're wearing any."

I am, but only to encourage that rough touch. "Find out for yourself."

Without a clasp to stop them, Sloane has my bra off in a blink, baring me from the waist up. Their mouth finds one breast and sucks, sending a lightning bolt of sensation straight to my clit, nipple hardening under the tight pressure of their lips. The other receives equal attention as blunt nails draw a slow, possessive line down my ribs. When I try and find a grip in the crown of their hair, Sloane shifts, taking the tangle of my dress with them as they sink to both knees in front of the bed.

I shudder at the tease of their hair across my stomach, light as a paintbrush, right as Sloane's tongue follows the curve of my hip in another blazing stroke. My only warning before the damp silk between my thighs is shredded is a wicked flash in green eyes, the ruin of my underwear tossed aside before they take a deep breath in, mouth an inch from the trimmed line of blonde curls.

"You don't get to play pillow princess, jewel," Sloane declares, seizing my hips and pulling me to the edge of the bed, at the mercy of gravity and their grip. "Touch yourself. Give me a show."

If it was anyone else, I would just push their head between my legs and tell them to behave, but the first time I tried that with Sloane, they held me on edge for nearly an hour until I sobbed for mercy. I sit up just enough for them to see me, cupping my breasts and giving both a firm squeeze, savoring the sudden thrum of heat under my skin. To be on display, opened up and eager, tugs at an old thread of fear —*vulnerable*—but Sloane won't let me fall.

I trade that trust with a moan when Sloane parts me using a slow stroke of their tongue, exposing the slick folds of my cunt to open air. They're so damn methodical, sucking every part of me into their mouth until I'm dripping, unable to stop my hips from jerking forward and demanding even more. To be treated like a delicacy, not a single drop spared, unravels me even more than the brand of Sloane's grip on my ass, holding me in place and daring me to endure.

"More," I gasp, pinching my nipples to hard, aching points.

"Good girls give specifics," Sloane says, holding my gaze as they draw swift circles around my clit. When I shiver, their fingers tighten in turn, and I suddenly remember that threat to spank me red. "More what, Jill?"

"I want you inside me."

"Mm, no points for being vague." Their tongue sweeps

over my entrance, too fast for me to clench tight and steal true pleasure from it. "Guess you don't want it enough."

My jaw drops, but protest is impossible when Sloane won't stop touching me. Their shoulders push my knees as wide as they can go, palms drawing a measured path down my thighs and back again, feather-light before massaging into taut muscle. Every slick kiss over my cunt is a torment, never lingering quite long enough, sparks of bliss refusing to catch into the flame I need. Sloane's gaze remains on my face, watching my patience fray as each attempt I make to ride their mouth goes unanswered, release held an inch out of reach.

"Jesus, Sloane." The words come out as a whimper, but I can't help myself. "Fuck me with your cock before I lose my mind."

Their amused hum verges on sadistic. "No."

Before I can whine, plead, or so much as breathe, Sloane drops every pretense of *slow* and *gentle*. They devour me with swift flicks against my clit and deep thrusts of their tongue, only to take me fully between their lips and suck so hard a burst of ecstasy leaves me breathless. After so much teasing, overstimulation puts every thought out of my head except gasping curses and their name, trying to resist their grip for just a little more friction before I finally—

"God, please, please, fuck—"

Orgasm is a golden thread pulled taut through my entire body, back arching as I throw my head towards the ceiling. A groan of delight from Sloane vibrates where I'm most sensitive, drawing the peak even higher before I collapse onto the bed, twisting against the sheets. I can hear how wet I am, the obscene path of their tongue written twice over in the air, until it's simply too much.

"Sloane, I can't..." The words come out winded;

aftershocks of ecstasy keep pulsing through me, refusing to relent.

"You could," they counter, only to pull away a breath later. "But there's something else you want, isn't there?"

I drag them upward without a word, undoing the last buttons of Sloane's shirt without a care for where each one goes. A few stitches tear when I wrench the garment off sculpted shoulders, but they don't comment, too occupied with unbuckling their belt the second both hands are free. Under hotel lights, the bruising across their chest is a wild, dark watercolor, tapering down past their heart.

I won't risk touching there, so I draw my fingertips down the hard core of muscle along Sloane's stomach, to where their length is trapped under silken briefs. Even that cursory touch makes their eyes flutter, but I resist the urge to stroke them again, because I need them naked—now.

Sloane's cock is hard and lovely under my hand, its thick head curving back towards their stomach, tip glistening with unspent desire. When I firm up my grip, a rebellious spark ignites in green eyes, breath catching in their throat.

"You haven't changed," they whisper. "Give an inch and you take a mile."

I smirk. "That's far more than an inch. I could count if you like."

Their response is to break my grip and yank both wrists over my head, strong enough to make me shiver. Sloane displaces the tangle of my legs with their own, spreading me wide again. Even the light pressure of their shaft against the outside of my cunt makes me bite my lip, the warmth and weight promising what's to come.

Sloane pauses, the mask of dominance on their face displaced by concern. "Are you still on birth control?"

"Yes," I say, and their shoulders instantly relax. "It seemed prudent."

I never ended up pursuing anyone else, but there was always a fantasy in the back of my mind, hoping Sloane and I would meet again, and maybe the pain between us would spill over in the way desire had, once upon a time. Yet no matter how primal the urge, I couldn't have a plan without a dose of practical protection. Neither of us want children; I'd never risk an accident getting in the way of that.

They grin. "Maybe there is a god."

My laugh echoes theirs before I lean against their grip, capturing Sloane's mouth in a searing kiss. "Yes, and she says, 'fuck me until I can't walk.'"

"Why, Ms. Rhodes," Sloane's eyes glint, gem-sharp. "It would be my pleasure."

The sudden dip into formality gets me laughing again, and I'm breathless when they sink into me, slow and steady. I ease into the stretch with a sigh, savoring the simple feeling of our bodies being joined, and wonder how the hell I didn't chase them across the planet the morning after I woke up to an empty bed. Fear is the answer, but it pales in comparison to the here-and-now, the notion that this is exactly how we're meant to be.

I hook my legs around Sloane's hips, keeping them close as they find a rhythm. Above me, inside me, with a pace that feels like the sweetest kind of vengeance. When they kiss me, the angle of their body changes, pressing the head of their cock exactly where I need them. Their mouth left me wet, but now I'm soaked, held in place by rippling muscle and wicked intent, Sloane's passion at the very end of its leash.

"Keep your arms up there," they say.

"And if I don't?"

Sloane rebukes me with a harder thrust, the shock of

bliss forcing a moan from my lips. "Then I won't have a hand free to do this."

They reach between our bodies, left elbow braced on the sheets before clever fingers find the sensitive swell of my clit. I gasp, one bright pulse of pleasure melting into another, meeting every time Sloane's cock bottoms out inside me. Their tempo quickens into a demand, a claim, keeping me pinned down against the bed as if I'd ever try and escape. I grip the pillow until my hands ache, fighting every urge to spend the energy building under my skin into theirs, raking nails down Sloane's back until it's red as their hair.

I'm so damn sensitive, primed by my first orgasm for the next, but I want Sloane to come over the edge with me. Rocking my hips to meet theirs earns a groan—progress. The constant weave of tension between my cunt drawing them deep and my clit throbbing with its own pulse makes me tighten around them, and that lingering squeeze chases a curse from low in Sloane's throat. They bury their face in the curve of my neck, and I feel the second they unravel, a flood of white-hot release tipping me straight over into bliss.

Sloane keeps moving, whipping the ecstasy between us to even greater heights. I cry out as the world blurs at the edges, locking my legs around their hips until my body simply refuses to endure, limbs going slack as I pant for breath. They slow down in the wake of my collapse, face warm with the sheen of sweat, desire cutting a black centerpiece through the bright emerald of their eyes.

"Stay," I whisper the second I can form words again. "Please stay."

"I'm not going anywhere." Sloane bows their head to kiss me again. "I won't leave you, Jillian. I promise."

That almost breaks me. The scars around my heart twist in protest, warning what will happen if I give up this old protection, if I dare to trust Sloane a second time. But I take a breath and let the old pain fall away. It doesn't serve me anymore—if it ever did. Not every self-preservation reflex is worth the cost that comes after.

"Good." A choked, miserable syllable from the bottom of my throat, but Sloane doesn't hold me accountable for it. "Because I'm not done with you yet."

Sloane has a good sixty pounds on me, but my center of gravity is lower and intimately connected with theirs. I roll us both over in a flash, braced against their good shoulder. The trapped fire of their hair spills across the pillow, green eyes aglow with bliss, vivid against the multi-hued swell—cobalt, wine, marigold—of bruises on pale skin.

I trace around the shape of it, careful as I can be. Their pulse thumps under my fingertips, still laced with adrenaline. "Walker did a number on your heart, didn't she?"

"You're a better shot." They cover my hand, fingers angled like an arrow. "A bullet barely compares."

I could withdraw into myself, apologize, but I don't. This moment is ours to share and reckon with, bringing the ragged edges of our mistakes together so something new can heal in the aftermath.

"I might aim a little lower next time," I joke. They chuckle, teeth flashing in a smile. "Now that I have you all to myself."

"As long as you want me," they say.

Forever sounds like a good start. The gift of Sloane's heart is better than anything I could ever steal.

CHAPTER 22

SLOANE

When Jillian breaks the line of our bodies, I swallow a groan.

I'm still half-hard from the heat of her, and watching the slow, pearlescent drip between lithe thighs puts the impetus for more under my skin, keen as a blade.

She places a kiss below my collarbones, and I ask, "Where are you going?"

"Guess." Her voice is rich with amusement, golden afterglow. The next brush of her lips settles over my stomach; muscle tightens by reflex, and the hot line of Jillian's tongue finds the divots there, leaving taut skin slick. "You have one up on me."

Oh. "I wasn't keeping score."

Jillian folds herself down at the edge of the bed, my knees framing her shoulders before she wraps a hand around the base of my cock, still glistening with her arousal. "Neither am I, really. But it's a good excuse to see you come undone without getting... distracted."

That brief hitch in her voice tells me everything. "What distracted you the most? When I was tasting that gorgeous cunt of yours and you begged me to fuck you? Was it feeling me come inside you again, knowing I was going to take what I wanted when you weren't allowed to touch me? Don't be shy, jewel."

Her reply is a subtle pump up my length, meeting her mouth where soft lips wrap around the head and suck, drawing me in like an act of worship. Bliss spikes across my nerves when Jillian lets go, mouth wet, and says simply: "Yes."

Any attempt at wit is stoppered by the renewed rush of blood to my cock. "Touché."

I relax against the bed, unable to look away from her. Desire blooms in the pit of my stomach as I grip the sheets; if Jillian wants my hands on the back of her head, she'll put them there. Not that I can complain when I'm offered the full luxury of her mouth, tongue painting hot stripes around my shaft while slow strokes of her hand make up the difference, working lower until I brush against the back of her throat.

Such deliberate focus is my undoing. Years of clinging to the echo of a memory, fragile as chalk after time's touch blurs every line, left me unprepared to have her again, to be the sole target of Jillian's attention. She wants *me*, not some fantasy we conjured into the air together, arrows of illusion aimed at each other's hearts. I bite my tongue, trying not to fall over the edge so easily, but watching her is too much— and closing my eyes is unthinkable.

"Jillian—"

Her eyes seek mine, bright with hunger, piercing gaze shattering the last of my control. My hips jerk, staggered, as I spill into her mouth. She swallows, letting out a pleased hum around my cock, gripping the weight under the seal of her lips until I surrender every drop, pleasure singing through my body from head to toe. Another halcyon note makes me tremble as Jillian releases me, exposing every hot inch of skin to the cool air of the room.

I pull her up the bed for a breathless kiss, turning in against her body. She smiles as we fall into alignment, warm with languor. "Has our blood cooled off enough for an actual conversation yet?"

"Maybe," I joke. "What's on your mind?"

"That we should make a few new rules." Jillian's fingers idly walk up and down my stomach, dispelling a jolt of nerves. "If we're doing this, I want us to be honest with each other. *Really* honest. No deflecting the subject or assuming what the other person wants."

I nod. "I think we both need practice asking the hard questions."

"It's terrifying," she admits. "But I can't lose you again, Sloane. Being a coward already cost me too much."

"So did my pride." Both of us have a surplus; the same confidence attracting us to each other comes with hooks and barbs, eager to catch. "If I can't drop my guard around you, something's wrong."

"Agreed." Jillian sighs. "But we know better now. My slate's clean."

"So is mine." The hint of light outside our window catches my eye. "What time is it?"

"A bit after dawn, I think." Jillian stretches under the sheets before relaxing against my side. "We jumped ahead six hours across the Atlantic."

"Then I have a phone call to make."

I draw on some truly heroic willpower to leave the bed and grab the new burner phone from my bag, but at least I get to enjoy Jillian watching me on the way back. I crack

RIEN GRAY

open the box—it was a hundred-dollar sale from one of the airport vending machines—and hook up the charger near the bed before turning the phone on. The SIM only comes with a scant hour of international credit, but that's fine; ten minutes will be more than enough.

Zouch is an early riser. He answers after the first ring. "Hello? May I ask who's calling? This is a private line."

"You know who this is," I reply, "and I know you gave me up, Thomas."

"Sloane!" He gasps my name like it punched him in the chest. "Listen, listen. I had no choice. It was nothing personal. Interpol had the NCA tracking my accounts. They found everything. They were going to *take* everything."

"So you sold me out for a sweetheart deal." Unfortunately for Zouch, Denning hit a dead end. "Well, Thomas, I'm afraid you're still going to lose everything. Because I'm going to empty out your private vault. Every last painting, sculpture, and piece of jewelry. You'll never see it again."

He sputters. "You can't. They're still watching me. They'll catch you."

"They won't." I've had years to memorize his sprawl of a mansion. Dodging a few cars and cameras is child's play. "You use a Döttling security door, don't you? Silver and black finish. Six individual locks on the outside, seven-digit locking system."

His soft, shocked exhale tells me everything.

"You know how good I am, but guess what? When it comes to breaking and entering, my girlfriend's even better. Sixty seconds and she'll peel through that safe like a nice ripe orange."

Jillian's soft, wicked laugh makes me consider going for a round three.

"Sloane, please," he wheezes. "We can come to some kind of arrangement."

No, we can't. "Great doing business with you, Thomas."

I hang up and abandon the phone to the bedside table. Jillian curls up against my side, draping an arm over my ribs. "Girlfriend, was it?"

"I wasn't going to give him your name," I note. "Unless you want a different title?"

She makes a show of considering her answer. "'Queen of thieves' was nice."

"All right, your majesty." We're in the right country for it, at least. "So what does that make me?"

Jillian smiles. "Sovereign, maybe?"

I do like the sound of that. "Well, my queen, want to go ruin a millionaire's day?"

"Always. But first—" She shifts into the cradle of my arms, turning us to face the Thames outside, where London is just starting to wake up. "Let's steal a minute for us."

"More than a minute, if you like." I press a kiss to the top of golden hair. "I love you."

"I love you too."

Jillian says it with such joy, such relief. We have a lot of work between us to fix the damage of the last three years, but I'm not worried about the path ahead. She and I are the best in the world for a reason.

Anything in our way simply doesn't stand a chance.

ALSO BY RIEN GRAY

WANT MORE QUEER CRIMINALS IN CHICAGO?

Check out my Fatal Fidelity series:

Love Kills Twice

Love Bleeds Deep

Love Burns Bright

A Love So Dark

FIND ME ONLINE!

Newsletter: https://subscribepage.io/riengray
Website: www.riengray.com
Twitter: https://twitter.com/riengray

Printed in Great Britain
by Amazon

40841159R00108